"Just remember seen you use s

"Cowboy charm?" Ro[...]
sell whiskey to a teetotaler.

"Give Brooke that look that mesmerizes a woman, and makes her think you're going to grab her, toss her on your horse and ride off into the sunset."

"Do I do that for you?"

His warm, husky voice rippled through Elizabeth. He leaned forward in his chair. His strong gaze peered into her. He had the slightest smile on his face.

Oh, yeah, that was the look.

Horse and sunset here I come.

Dear Reader,

People frequently ask how I get my ideas. Often something in life piques my curiosity, and I go into "what if" mode. That's what happened with *Big City Cowboy*.

While in Estes Park for a wedding, my family and I went horseback riding. Our guide caught my attention, but not only because of his phenomenal looks. As he helped my middle son, a gentleman approached the cowboy about modeling. Afterwards, he said people often asked him to model and couldn't understand why he didn't jump at the opportunity.

My writer's imagination zoomed into overdrive. What if this cowboy was desperate and had to model? What would be important enough to make him leave the ranch and venture into the big city? The answer popped into my head—his mom. I added a feisty, career-driven woman who needed this private cowboy to be a household name, and Rory and Elizabeth's story came to life.

I never imagined at that wedding I'd achieve a lifelong dream—my first published novel. I hope you have as much fun reading Rory and Elizabeth's story as I had writing it. I'd love to hear from you. Visit me at www.juliebenson.net.

Julie

Big City Cowboy

Julie Benson

TORONTO NEW YORK LONDON
AMSTERDAM PARIS SYDNEY HAMBURG
STOCKHOLM ATHENS TOKYO MILAN MADRID
PRAGUE WARSAW BUDAPEST AUCKLAND

Recycling programs
for this product may
not exist in your area.

ISBN-13: 978-0-373-75385-7

BIG CITY COWBOY

Printed in U.S.A.

ABOUT THE AUTHOR

An avid daydreamer since childhood, Julie always loved creating stories. After graduating from the University of Texas at Dallas with a degree in sociology, she worked as a case manager before having her children: three boys—and many years later, she started pursuing a writing career to challenge her mind and save her sanity. Now she writes full-time in Dallas, where she lives with her husband, their sons, two lovable black dogs, two guinea pigs, a turtle and a fish. When she finds a little quiet time, which isn't often, she enjoys making jewelry and reading a good book.

To Kevin. Thanks for sticking with me through the ups and downs of life, and for believing in me and this dream. You're definitely a keeper.

To Dr. Angela Krause and David Goddard. Thanks for the wedding invitation and for introducing me to Estes Park. This story never would have happened without you two.

Chapter One

Estes Park, Colorado

"There is no way I'm getting on a horse."

Elizabeth Harrington-Smyth pulled into the Twin Creeks Ranch parking lot, vowing she'd never attend another wedding, not even her own should she ever make time to date. So far, being her cousin Janice's bridesmaid hadn't been the greatest experience. And don't get her started on the problems with the whole destination wedding idea that was the trend now.

"Estes Park is so beautiful, and what better way to see the scenery than going horseback riding?" Since moving to Denver three years ago, Janice had gone all outdoorswoman. Today she really fit the part, wearing jeans, a denim shirt and a red bandanna tied around her ebony ponytail.

Elizabeth shuddered. "Looking at the mountains as I sat in the hotel bar was good enough for me."

"I think this will be a great bridesmaid outing," chirped Laura, obedient bridesmaid number one. Her Katie Couric perkiness had overwhelmed Elizabeth within five minutes of meeting Janice's coworker.

"I was hoping we'd get time to go riding. It's something I've always wanted to try," chimed in Claire, perfect bridesmaid number two, as they spilled out of Janice's Camry. In addition to being a morning person, Claire had the irritating characteristics of being tall, slender and possessing a disgustingly high metabolism.

"I let you out of the hike yesterday because you were queasy and tired from the altitude, but I want us to have a good time together," Janice insisted. "It's girl bonding."

"The wedding party activities are half the fun of being a bridesmaid," Claire said.

According to whom? Clearly, Elizabeth and the rest of the bridal party had different definitions of fun.

Dust swirled around her, making her sneeze. It seemed as if they were surrounded by bales of hay. At least she'd taken a Claritin this morning, so she wouldn't look like a red-eyed monster due to raging allergies.

"My idea of a good time is having a massage, facial and pedicure at the hotel, not riding on a smelly horse." Elizabeth waved a fly away from her face. "The outdoors is pretty to look at, but I'm not keen on actually being *in* it. I'll wait here by this fence—"

"It's a corral, Elizabeth," Janice corrected.

"Then I'll wait here by the corral. The rest of you go ahead and enjoy."

"I've never ridden a horse, but I'm willing to be adventurous, Elizabeth," Laura coaxed.

"You're here, so you might as well come with us," Claire added.

"I'm afraid my Jimmy Choos aren't meant for horseback riding." Now that was an excuse any woman could understand and respect.

"Didn't I tell you to wear sensible shoes that you didn't mind getting dirty?" Janice asked.

Elizabeth stared at her cute leopard-print flats and her blood pressure rose. "All you said was wear sensible shoes, which I am. These *are* flats. I'd never have worn Jimmy Choos if you'd mentioned getting dirty."

"Sorry. I guess I must've forgotten the getting dirty part."

Janice flashed her an I'm-the-bride-forgive-me smile. "There are so many details to planning a large destination wedding. I'm surprised I haven't forgotten more things. You'll have to make the best of the situation now."

The cool March breeze blew a strong odor of horse manure Elizabeth's way. "Too late. It smells terrible out here. Flies are everywhere, and the quiet is driving me crazy. Everyone moves too slowly! I almost mowed over two people when I walked down to the hotel lobby to get coffee this morning."

"Exactly why you should join us," Claire insisted. "You need to slow down and learn to appreciate nature's gifts."

"I'm in advertising. *I* determine what people appreciate, not the other way around. And who says I don't appreciate nature?"

"You have to go, Elizabeth," her cousin whined. "I want *all* of us to go. This means so much to me."

Elizabeth bristled. "Isn't it enough that I took off work for your wedding when I've got a major ad campaign due? Between all the activities, the spotty internet service and a slight case of altitude sickness, I haven't gotten half the work done here that I need to."

Her job was hanging by a thread. Devlin Designs wanted to launch a new jeans campaign and she had the perfect one all mapped out, but couldn't find the right spokesman. On top of that, the contract for the remainder of Devlin's business was up for renewal soon. No spokesman, no new campaign, no contract renewals—and then she'd be out of a job.

"What an honor, you taking off work to come to my wedding," Janice snapped.

Laura and Claire slid a few feet away, obviously wanting to avoid the awkward conversation.

In addition to the wedding, Elizabeth had hoped to spend a little time with her parents, who were flying in, as well. But when she'd checked her voice mail after arriving in Denver she'd learned they weren't coming.

"I'm sorry, Janice, really. I'm out of sorts. Did Mom and Dad tell you they've headed off to some mountain in Germany on an archeological dig? I haven't seen them in forever, and though I shouldn't be, I'm pretty disappointed."

"No. How could they do that at the last minute? Don't they know we'll have to pay for their dinners whether they're here or not?"

Elizabeth shrugged. "They said a bone flute and an erotic figurine had been discovered there. If these pieces are authentic, it'll be the best example Upper Paleolithic art ever. They insisted they absolutely couldn't pass this up."

"They say that about every dig."

"You think I'd be used to their last-minute cancellations by now." Elizabeth smiled weakly. This kind of parental disinterest and disappointment had filled her life for as long as she could remember. "Then there's work. My job's on the line with this campaign."

"Come on, Elizabeth. You're not going to lose your job. They'd have to hire three people to replace you," Janice said.

"We're on the verge of losing a client that represents over half of our business." Her cousin didn't realize how precarious the advertising business was.

Elizabeth was good at what she did. She knew this crazy ad world well. No one had given her the management supervisor job; she'd earned it. She'd started at the bottom and from there studied the market, worked hard, learned from her superiors and was the ultimate team player. She gave two hundred percent without being asked, and had eventually secured her current position. Unfortunately, sometimes hard work counted for squat.

"If we lose this account the company will have no choice but to lay off a lot of people, including me, since it was my account."

"Work is all that matters to you." Janice crossed her arms

over her chest. "You're a workaholic. You always have been. You're just like your parents."

Ouch. "I am not, and that's a low blow."

"You need to get some balance in your life," Janice continued, shifting into sympathetic mode. "You're all work and no play. You need to date. Have fun."

Elizabeth winced, knowing where the conversation was headed. Why did every married or engaged person feel they possessed a sacred duty to impart relationship advice to single relatives and friends? "Work is so crazy right now I don't have much time for anything, especially dating."

"Is it a time issue, or is it because no guy meets enough requirements on your ridiculous checklist?"

"It's not silly. I have to know what qualities I want in a partner, and what things are deal breakers."

"You'll be surprised how fast you'll throw out that list when you find the right guy."

Elizabeth had begun to think the right guy for her didn't exist. Or if he did, she worried she wouldn't find him without a map and a guide.

She grabbed a deep, calming breath. "Can we start over? I know I haven't been the most fun lately. We've had one round of layoffs already at work, and with this client halfway out the door, I'm way past stressed out."

"It's really that bad?" Janice asked, genuinely concerned.

She nodded.

"I'm sorry my wedding turned out to be poor timing for you." Janice reached out and clasped her hand. "I appreciate you being here, considering what's going on with you. Is the altitude sickness getting any better?"

Biting her lip to hold back her emotions over her cousin's unexpected empathy, Elizabeth nodded. "I'm tired and a bit queasy, but I can handle it, as long as it doesn't get worse."

"Look at that gorgeous cowboy walking our way," Claire

said, popping up beside them. "Not that your wedding isn't reason enough, but this guy makes the entire trip worthwhile."

Janice squeezed Elizabeth's hand and let go. "Yum-oh." Her face lit up like Times Square after dark. "Elizabeth, you've got to see this guy. He's behind you a few feet. Turn, but don't be obvious that you're looking."

Behind her in the corral stood an attractive cowboy. His dark brown hat cast a shadow over his face, but didn't conceal his strong jaw or classic cheekbones. Dressed in a simple navy button-down shirt, jeans, chaps complete with leather fringe and dusty cowboy boots, he was the real deal.

"I'd be willing to risk getting hay in all sorts of awkward places for a little time alone in the barn with him," Claire said.

"Close your mouth, Janice, or you'll start catching flies," Elizabeth teased. "Plus you're getting married tomorrow."

"That doesn't mean I'm dead. I can still appreciate the exceptional scenery."

Elizabeth shook her head. "Sure he's good-looking, but what's so fantastic about a cowboy? I don't get it. They smell like horses. They spend a good part of their days cleaning manure out of barn stalls. What about that inspires romance?"

Claire looked ready to tackle the cowboy. "They're so rugged. So strong."

"Janice Rogers and party," cowboy hottie called out in a lazy drawl.

"That's me, or us, rather." Janice waved her hand and gave him a big smile.

"Let's see about getting you ladies on some horses." He pointed to Claire. "Come with me."

Claire beamed and practically ran over Laura to get to the cowboy. Then she introduced herself, giggled and tossed her hair.

Elizabeth laughed. Watching this show unfold might be fun, after all.

The ranch hand tilted his hat and nodded. "Rory."

"Even his name's gorgeous," Laura crooned dreamily to no one in particular.

"Clem, help this lady with Biscuit."

Claire slowly started moving toward an older cowboy, but kept glancing over her shoulder at Rory all doe-eyed.

Then he motioned to Janice, who stepped on Elizabeth's foot in her haste to reach him.

"Watch it," Elizabeth snapped.

"Sorry," her cousin said, but her gaze remained locked on the cowboy. If he offered to sell her the Rocky Mountains right now, she'd be whipping out her MasterCard.

Wait a minute. Elizabeth smiled. That's exactly what she wanted people to do—open their wallets. *Thank you, Lord, for sending the answer to my prayers.* She just might be able to pull this campaign out of the fire.

When she'd proposed that Devlin Designs center its men's jeans campaign on a cowboy, she'd had this type of female reaction in mind. Micah Devlin liked the idea, but not the models she'd suggested. Now she understood what he'd meant about something being missing in all the models dressed like cowboys. They weren't *authentic*.

Bingo. Yes, sir. Rory could be the answer to all her problems.

By the time he motioned her forward, she had a tentative pitch mentally mapped out.

"I hope the horse knows what he's doing, because I don't have a clue," she joked as an icebreaker. Starting her conversation with, "Come to New York to model designer jeans," seemed a little abrupt. She needed to loosen the guy up first. Appear to be interested in his life here in the great outdoors.

"As long as you hold on to the reins and sit up straight, you'll be okay. We haven't lost anyone yet."

"Elizabeth might be the first." Janice laughed. "She's not exactly athletic."

Rory looked her up and down with eyes that were liquid

gold. She could feel herself blush, something she hadn't done in years.

"She looks like she can handle herself well enough."

Apparently chivalry wasn't as dead as everyone believed.

"Put your left foot in the stirrup," Rory said as he pointed toward the saddle. "Then grab hold of the saddle horn with your right hand and pull up while you swing your leg over."

She glanced at the horse, an amazingly large one, and then back at Rory. The man had to be kidding. "Have you noticed how big the horse is, and how short I am? There's no way I can get up there."

"You are a little thing," he said, smiling.

Again, she blushed. This blushing was getting a little out of control.

"I'll help you."

How, exactly? She pictured this gorgeous man pushing her butt to shove her into the saddle. Could this experience get more humiliating?

She'd get on the horse on her own if it killed her. After placing her foot in the stirrup, she grabbed the saddle horn. Then she pushed off with her right foot and pulled as hard as she could. She was about to swing her leg over the saddle when she started slipping back down. Then she felt Rory's firm hands on her rear end, and next thing she knew, she was sitting on the horse.

Now she wished she hadn't skipped so many Pilates classes lately.

A minute later they headed off down a path into the great outdoors. The trees formed a canopy around them as they rode. The mountains loomed, harsh and demanding, making her feel incredibly insignificant.

Birds chirped. Wind rustled through the leaves. A stream babbled past. How did people stand the quiet?

Flies swarmed around her and the horse. She wanted to swat at them, but feared she'd fall off if she took one hand from the reins. To keep her mind off the insects and her already scream-ing thigh muscles, she focused on Rory at the front of their little caravan. The set of his shoulders spoke of his confidence. He moved in the saddle with a casual grace. Everything about him said how comfortable he was in his own skin. Then there was his voice as he tossed out tidbits about the area and its history. Slow, melodic and deep, it wrapped around her like a warm hug.

Rory pointed to the towering oak to his left. "That's our wishing tree. If you make a wish and circle the tree three times, your wish will come true. Feel free to hop down and make a wish while we're here."

Laura and Claire immediately vaulted off their horses, dashed to the tree and circled it three times. "What did you wish for?" Janice called out as she joined her friends.

"I wished to find someone as wonderful as David," Laura chirped, referring to Janice's fiancé.

Claire giggled. "I wished Michael would propose."

Janice dashed around the tree. "I wish that I'll always be as happy as I am right now."

Why did people wish for things like that? Only the foolish wished for something impossible.

"What about you?" Rory asked. He'd dismounted, and now stood beside Elizabeth.

Even if she were willing to get off her horse and risk need-ing Rory to give her another boost into the saddle, the only thing she'd wish for was landing him as a spokesman for the jeans campaign. Wishing wouldn't make that happen. She'd rely on her business skills to accomplish it.

"I think I'll pass."

"Come on, Elizabeth, make a wish," Janice coaxed. "What could it hurt?"

If only her cousin knew.

The remainder of the ride passed in a blur of trees, rocks and mountains. Three hours later, when they returned to the corral, Elizabeth didn't like the outdoors any better, but she knew her instincts about Rory had been dead on. He'd make the perfect spokesperson for Devlin Designs men's jeans. He spun a good tale, which would work well in TV commercials, and then there were his looks and the way he moved. A guy either had a presence or he didn't, and Rory had it in spades.

"I'm a management supervisor at Rayzor Sharp Media. It's an advertising agency," she said, ignoring her protesting muscles when he helped her off the horse. "You'd be the perfect model for one of my clients. You have a presence that can't be taught or faked, while you're real enough to connect with the average man."

He laughed. Not a good sign.

"I'm not interested, but thanks for asking."

"It's a major national campaign. The exposure would be excellent."

"Doesn't matter."

She reached into her purse, pulled out a business card and held it out to him. "You could get a free trip to New York out of the deal."

"Right now all I'm interested in is getting this horse taken care of," he said as he reached for the reins.

Her stubbornness kicked up a notch. She couldn't give up when so much rode on this campaign and Rory's participation.

"Elizabeth, hurry up," Janice yelled from the parking lot.

"Lady, the rest of your party's ready to go."

Let 'em wait. "Did I mention the job will pay around thirty thousand dollars? Surely a ranch hand like you could use the money."

Rory pushed his hat off his forehead a bit. Now she had his attention.

Dark coffee-colored eyes peered down at her. The look in those eyes could sell refrigerators to Eskimos. Or hopefully, designer jeans to the average man. Or the average man's significant other.

Then gravel crunched under car tires, drawing his gaze away from her. When his attention returned a moment later, his interest had vanished.

"Lady, the next tour group has pulled into the parking lot, and I don't have time for this."

She held out her card again. "If I agree to leave, will you take my contact info, and consider my business proposal?"

"Deal." Rory snatched the card out of her hand and shoved it in his shirt pocket. "But don't count on hearing from me."

That was okay. She believed in positive thinking. If she sent good karma into the world, good things would return to her. Now if she could only collect by getting Rory to agree to model—because she needed this cowboy or she was out of a job.

THREE DAYS LATER Rory sat in his worn leather desk chair as the banker he'd known all his life told him he couldn't approve a second mortgage.

"Rory, if things were different, if we were still a family-owned bank, maybe I could approve this, but I've got stock-holders to answer to. Twin Creeks carries too much debt to justify another loan."

He thanked John, reassured him that he understood it was simply a business decision, and hung up the phone.

Rory's chin sank to his chest. He'd already tried to sell some of their horses, but most folks were having financial difficulties, too. He'd looked for extra work, but there were too many unemployed people out there and no one was adding on help anyway. The second mortgage had been his last palatable choice to get the cash his mom needed. There had to be something he could do—his mom's life depended on it.

The McAlister family had gone through their savings to pay for the medical bills when Rory's dad had suffered a heart attack behind the wheel and sent his truck into a ditch, putting him and Rory's younger brother, Griffin, into the hospital. Then two years ago, when his dad's heart finally gave out, Rory cashed in most of their stocks to pay for those bills and his dad's funeral. Now, their mom had gone as far as she could with her cancer treatments and was left with one alternative, which turned out to be experimental—and expensive.

You have another alternative. You just don't like it.

He pulled open his middle desk drawer, shoved aside some papers and located Elizabeth Harrington-Smyth's business card.

He twirled it between his fingers as he stared out the window. The snow-capped Rocky Mountains filled his view. Though he'd seen them every day of his life, their beauty never failed to amaze him. Some people thought they had a magnificent view when they looked out at a city skyline. Personally, he didn't understand the appeal. Give him what God had created any day. Man's creations were strictly amateur in comparison.

His hands tightened around the chair arm and the worn leather creaked in protest. Visions of his dad sitting in this same chair flashed in Rory's mind. He still missed the old man every day. More so lately, since the doctor had found the inoperable tumor on his mother's brain. How he wished he could talk to his dad about what to do, even though he knew what his dad would say. *Do whatever's necessary to get the money for your mother. She's a good woman, the rock of this family, and she damned well deserves every shot to beat cancer.*

Knowing his mom had only one alternative didn't make this call any easier. Rory willed his hand to reach for the phone.

Nothing.

Not even a twitch.

Picking up a phone. Such a simple action, so why couldn't he?

Because this call would change his life irrevocably. But at least it was his choice, as opposed to bankers and doctors calling the shots. Life was full of choices. Some turned out well and some sucked pond water. All a body could do was think things through, make a careful decision and deal with any fallout.

The last thing Rory wanted to do was leave this ranch, even short-term. He loved the land, the horses and the hard work that made his muscles ache at the end of the day. He loved the mental challenge of managing the ranching business.

A quiet knock sounded on his office door. "Come in, Mom."

"How'd you know it was me?"

He smiled. "The ranch hands and Griff knock loud enough to break down the door. Avery rarely bothers to knock."

His mom grinned, but weariness filled her eyes, twisting his gut as she walked across the office. Until the last year she'd been active and energetic. Then she'd started chemo. The constant nausea had almost killed her, but hadn't done anything to shrink the tumor. Now, thanks to the steroids the doctor prescribed and her lack of energy for the long walks she enjoyed, her weight had ballooned. At least her hair had grown out enough for her to wear it in a short, spiky style. Despite all that, she hadn't given up. Talk about strong.

Her quiet strength always amazed him. She never complained, and remained positive. He'd always loved his mom, but now he admired her in a different way.

Rory said a silent prayer that this experimental treatment would work.

"Griffin is ready to take me and Avery to the airport." His mom stopped in front of his desk. Her frail hand rested on his forearm. "Are you sure we can afford this treatment, since insurance isn't covering it? It's so expensive."

Thank goodness for Avery. His little sister, who'd always driven him crazy, wanting to tag along with him and his friends, had turned out okay. Since their mother's diagnosis, she'd stepped into the family caretaker role. Avery coordinating their mom's appointments and accompanying her had allowed Rory to focus on putting food on the table and keeping the ranch afloat. He couldn't ask for a better sister.

"Don't worry about the money, Mom. I've got the situation under control."

She squeezed his arm and peered down at him. For a moment he worried that she'd read the lie in his eyes.

"If you're absolutely sure."

"I'll worry about the finances. You concentrate on getting well." He stood, walked around his desk and enveloped her in a hug, wishing he could take on this fight for her.

He couldn't bear to lose her, too. Not so soon after losing his dad.

She kissed him on the cheek, and he pulled away. "Now, get out of here. I don't want you to miss your flight."

Once his mother had closed the door behind her, Rory returned to his desk. He picked up the business card, flipped open his cell phone and dialed.

Chapter Two

"Elizabeth Harrington-Smyth."

Her voice sounded exactly as Rory remembered—pushy, businesslike and New York City. At the ranch she'd been like a defensive lineman, single-minded in pursuit of her goal, intent on getting to him, the quarterback. The lady definitely didn't acknowledge the word *no*. Not exactly his favorite type of woman.

"It's Rory McAlister. We met when you were at Twin Creeks Ranch in Estes Park last weekend. I was your guide on the horseback ride."

"I remember, though I'm surprised to hear from you."

That made two of them.

He swallowed hard and barreled forward. "The modeling job you said you could get me, is it still available?"

"Yes, it is."

"And it'll pay thirty thousand dollars?"

"Over the course of the campaign, yes."

"What does that mean?"

"You'll get paid when we do the photo shoots. Then you get paid again whenever the material is used for an aspect of the campaign."

He needed to do some research to see if he could work a deal to get more money up front. "Are you interested?"

"Yes." He forced the word past the lump in his throat.

"Email me a photograph of yourself as soon as we get off the phone. My address is on my card."

"I don't have anything taken by a professional photographer." Nor would he, if he had to pay for them.

"I don't care. Send me what you've got, even if it's family photos. If you have ones showing your face clearly, that would be great."

"I'll send what I can find."

"Have you gotten an agent yet?"

Forget that. An agent would take a percentage of what he made. No way would he give anyone a part of his money, when he needed every penny so desperately. Surely with an MBA he could negotiate the deal. "I'm representing myself."

"I want you on the first available flight to New York."

"You expecting me to pay for the flight?"

"We'll reimburse you. Put the ticket on your credit card and turn in your receipt to me. I'll send it on to Accounting, and they'll cut you a check within two weeks."

"I can't do that." He'd hit his credit limit paying for the two plane tickets to Portland.

"If that's a problem, I'll contact our travel person to book your flight."

"You do that."

"I'll email you the details."

"What about a hotel? I'm not paying for that, either."

She paused, and he imagined her sitting at a clean desk in an efficiently organized office, trying to decide if he'd be this big a pain about everything. He made a mental note not to push her too much on anything but money. That issue was nonnegotiable. He had to pinch pennies.

"I'll book you at a hotel near our office. I'll email you the details. Is that to your satisfaction?"

"I'll see you tomorrow."

For better or worse, his life was about to change.

ELIZABETH HUNG UP HER PHONE, jumped out of her chair, took two quick steps across her office, then stopped. A management supervisor who planned on becoming a vice president did not dash into the hallway because she was excited. She sucked in a calming breath, smoothing the front of her black pencil skirt, and headed for her friend Chloe Walsh's office.

Reaching it, Elizabeth shuddered at the clutter surrounding her. Piles of paper dotted the room. She couldn't even see the top of Chloe's desk because of the stacks of portfolios and pictures on it. Elizabeth shook her head. How did her best friend find anything or get any work done? This office would drive her past the brink of insanity.

"I heard from cowboy hottie," Elizabeth said as she sank into the chair in front of Chloe's desk—once she'd transferred a stack of photos from the seat to the floor.

"The gorgeous ranch hand from Colorado?" Chloe pointed to the picture Janice had taken of Rory during the week of a million bridesmaid events.

"That's our guy," Elizabeth said. "A real-life cowboy dream, if you liked the rough outdoorsman type. He called me back."

Chloe swiveled her chair around and glanced out her tenth-floor Madison Avenue window.

"What're you doing?"

"I'm checking for pigs. I swore they'd be flying if that cowboy ever called you back."

"Me, too. Thankfully, we were both wrong." Elizabeth plucked a piece of lint off her skirt. "We've got to get moving full blast on finalizing the idea. We need to finish storyboards, ideas for TV commercials, print ad mock-ups, billboard ideas, and have everything ready ASAP. Then when we do Rory's photo shoot we'll be set to present everything to Micah Devlin."

"What'll we do if Devlin doesn't go for this idea?"

"Don't even think it. Be positive. We have to believe in this campaign and sell him on it."

"Got it, Chief. I'll be Little Miss Sunshine."

"Let's not go overboard. The guy's smart. Devlin won't buy a snow job. We'll believe in the campaign because it's going to be wonderful."

"I'll make a note of that." Chloe grabbed a scrap of paper and pen off the nearest pile and started writing. "Be positive, but not delusional."

Elizabeth smiled. What would she do without Chloe? Her friend always made her laugh when she needed to most. "It's scary how much rides on this idea."

"You didn't tell our cowboy that, did you?"

"Do I look stupid? If he knew how important this campaign is, and how central he is to pulling it off, who knows how much he'd want to get paid."

Chloe held up her hands in mock defeat. "Excuse me for losing my mind and forgetting you're all business no matter what the situation or how gorgeous the guy. Surely if he wanted too much money we could find another cowboy."

Elizabeth took another calming breath, needing to channel her nervousness. "I've tried. It's not as easy as it sounds. Believe it or not, most cowboys just want to spend time on their horses riding the range, or whatever it is they do. Plus there's something about this guy."

"Other than good looks?"

"There's something about the way he moves. He exudes confidence."

"If he's a real cowboy, and all they want to do is ride the range, why's this guy willing to model?"

Elizabeth had asked herself the same question since Rory's call. "I don't care, as long as he is."

When she'd given him her card he'd been polite, but she'd seen the you've-got-to-be-kidding look in his eyes. She'd suspected modeling was the last thing he would do, right after moving away from Colorado.

So why the major about-face?

Well, there was no reason to borrow trouble when what had changed his mind wasn't important. All that mattered was that she got what she needed for the campaign.

"We better hope he doesn't change his mind," Chloe said.

"Again, I say, don't even think it. Think positive, because I don't know about you, but I don't want to be on the unemployment line."

"You think Devlin's that close to pulling his business?"

"He made it quite clear when I talked to him yesterday that his patience has run out. He's given me to the end of the week to find a spokesman, so we're doing whatever we have to in order to get this done. We've got to finalize this campaign fast or we'll all be out of a job."

ELIZABETH STARED AT Rory's face displayed on her computer monitor. No doubt about it, he was a natural. Despite the amateur photos, the camera loved him. His maleness oozed through the screen. He would be the perfect spokesman.

Women would take one look at Rory in Devlin's designer jeans and buy a pair for their guy. Men would wear the jeans hoping they'd look like Rory, and have women falling at their feet. Exactly what the client wanted. Their jeans sold well in New York and Los Angeles, but hadn't broken into other major markets. Devlin wanted to get the guys who wore Levi's and Wranglers to spend their hard-earned cash on his expensive product. Rory could pry open those wallets.

She spun around in her desk chair, giddy over how things were coming together. She couldn't wait to show Devlin the mock-up. If he didn't like Rory and the campaign, then fine, let him take his business elsewhere, because nothing would please the man.

She considered sending Devlin Rory's photos, but her practical nature balked at the idea. Instinct told her to wait until she had the campaign completely outlined and professional photographs of Rory. God forbid she sold Devlin on the cowboy, and then discovered Rory froze in front of a camera.

Needing to stretch her legs and energize her mind, Elizabeth decided to take a quick bathroom break and then grab a fresh cup of coffee before she dived into the details for Rory's photo session.

She weaved her way through the maze of offices and cubicles until she reached the woman's restroom, where quiet sobs floated toward her from the middle stall. She knocked gently on the door. "You okay?"

"I'm fine." More sobs contradicted the words.

"Nancy? What's wrong?"

The door latch clicked free, and Nancy, a friend and fellow management supervisor, exited the stall. The middle-aged woman clutched a wad of toilet paper in each hand, and her eyes were red and swollen.

"Everything's not fine. Tell me what's wrong."

Racking sobs consumed her. Not sure of what else to do, Elizabeth enveloped the woman in an embrace.

"I found out yesterday that I have breast cancer," Nancy choked out, once her crying subsided.

You have breast cancer. One of the most feared phrases a woman could hear. Tears pooled in Elizabeth's own eyes for this woman, and what she was facing. "I'm so sorry, Nancy." She tightened her hold on her friend. "If you want to go home, I'll say you weren't feeling well."

Nancy stepped out of Elizabeth's embrace and dabbed at her eyes with the toilet paper. "Let me think about it. I'm not sure I want to go home. It's so lonely there. I kept saying there was time for me to have a family. I said I'd focus on that once I felt secure in my career." Her voice cracked. "Now I've got nothing but my career, and because of the cancer, I may never have the chance to get married."

"They've made great strides in breast cancer treatment. It's not the death sentence it once was." Elizabeth's words sounded so hollow, when women still died of breast cancer every day.

"From your mouth to God's ears. They want me to have surgery next week and start chemo soon after that."

"Do you need someone to go with you?"

"I'll let you know. Right now I'm in shock." She sighed deeply. "I think I will take the day off. I'll call my best friend and see if she wants to go out for lunch. Then we can do some shopping therapy."

As Elizabeth returned to her office, she heard her blaring phone from halfway down the hall. Once seated at her desk, she glanced at caller ID. Micah Devlin. So much for having everything in order before she talked to him. Taking a deep breath, she picked up her phone.

"I'm glad you called, Micah." She tried not to wince over her white lie. "I've found the perfect man for your campaign, but I won't have photos for you until after the shoot tomorrow."

"Send me what you have."

"They're family pictures. I'd prefer to wait for the professional shots."

"Send them. I want to see this guy to make sure we're on the right track this time."

Elizabeth winced at Devlin's reminder of her previous suggestions for a spokesperson. Ones he had immediately, and not so politely, shot down. Some clients were dreams to work with. She had plenty of those, and they kept her sane and confident. Micah Devlin could benefit from a class on how to tactfully get his point across without incinerating those who worked for him.

"I have every confidence you'll be as pleased with this choice as I am."

She retrieved Rory's message from her email, hit Forward and typed Devlin's name. After saying a quick prayer, she hit Send.

Here goes everything.

"I'm emailing his photos to you right now. Keep in mind these aren't professionally done, but I believe his essence, his personality, comes through nonetheless."

She heard Devlin's computer keys clicking as he retrieved her message. She couldn't breathe. Thoughts bounced around in her brain. She hadn't updated her résumé in years. How would she tell her parents if she lost her job? She had mortgage payments....

"Now that's what I'm talking about. He's somebody the average man can relate to. He's not one of those pretty boy models. Before I sign him, I want to see how he comes off in a professional shoot."

Air rushed into Elizabeth's lungs, and she smiled over passing the first hurdle. "Rory will be in town tomorrow, and by Friday's meeting we'll have photos for you."

"I've contacted Harms and Finn."

Devlin's little tact problem reared its ugly head again. So that's why he'd called—to drop that bomb. Her firm, Rayzor Sharp Media, had lost an account to them six months ago. The agency was top-notch and hungry. "They're good."

"I meet with them tomorrow."

"Then I look forward to showing you what we've got on Friday."

She could pull this campaign together. If she didn't sleep until after the meeting, lived on Starbucks with double shots, and the rest of her team did the same, they'd be fine.

No problem.

Except that they were working with a cowboy, not a professional model. A total unknown who'd never modeled before. The unknown made Elizabeth nervous. It was always so unpredictable.

RORY SAT IN HIS OFFICE waiting for his brother. Things were moving much faster than he'd expected. When he'd called Elizabeth he'd never dreamed she would expect him to be on the first flight to New York. She was probably one of those people who stayed attached to the office via her iPhone so she never missed a message, even when she was supposed to be on vacation. Life was way too short to spend it that attached to anything but family.

He smiled. At least he wouldn't be the only one miserable. Having to manage the ranch would severely cramp Griff's style. The life of the party, his kid brother never turned down an invitation, but would soon discover he couldn't be out all night and sleep until noon while running the ranch.

Rory glanced up as he sauntered in and flung himself into the leather wing chair in the corner of the office. Griffin had a gift with animals, especially horses. He had a way of calming them, sensing when something was wrong. Business was an entirely different matter. Despite his ability in math, Griffin hadn't shown any interest in learning that side of the ranch. All that was about to change. Little brother was going to have to step up.

"I couldn't get the second mortgage."

"Why?"

"The downturn in the economy has caused a drop in tourism. Pair that with the amount of debt Twin Creeks already carries, and John couldn't justify it."

"You'd think since he was dad's best friend, he'd cut us a little slack."

"John's a smart businessman, and this was purely a business decision."

"Wait a minute. Mom and Avery left for Portland yesterday. How did you pay for their flights?"

"I put it on a credit card." One charging a fortune in interest. The hole Rory was digging kept getting deeper. "I need to get additional cash coming in before we start receiving Mom's medical bills."

"Did you tell her?"

Rory shook his head. "I didn't tell Avery, either. She isn't to know anything about this. No one is, for that matter. This stays between you and me. Are you clear on that?"

"But if—"

"Avery's got to take care of Mom. That's her job, keeping her calm and positive. You mention any of this, and I'll beat you to within an inch of your life. You got that, little brother?"

Griffin nodded.

"I've got the money situation under control, but I need you to take over the ranch's day-to-day operations."

"I'm obviously missing something. How did you find a way to come up with that kind of cash?"

"I'm going to New York City to model."

Griffin laughed. "No, seriously, Rory. What're we going to do?"

"This isn't a joke. I called the advertising executive who was here last week. She's got a client I can work for who will pay thirty grand for me to do an advertising campaign. I'm leaving tonight."

"What? Are you sure about this? You hate being in the spotlight, and you hate having your picture taken. If anything, you've always tried to blend into the background."

"What choice do I have? If Mom doesn't get this treatment, she'll die."

Griffin nodded, and for a moment the weight of their worry hung in the air.

"You have to hold things together here while I'm in New York."

"Tell me what to do."

Some of the heaviness pressing on Rory's chest lifted. He picked up a three-ring binder and gave Griff a crash course on Twin Creeks' finances.

"Don't spend money on anything but the essentials, Griff. I've cut expenses to the bone. In doing that I haven't had to let anyone go."

"It's that bad?"

"We're not on the verge of bankruptcy, but things are tight." Rory handed over a file. "Jameson is interested in buying Star's foal. Follow up with him next week. He's been lowballing us. I've given him the best price possible. Don't let him haggle with you. Another copy of the quote I gave him is in his file."

"Everything sounds simple enough."

"Stick to the budget." Rory flipped to another section in the binder.

"Thank goodness for cell phones. You're only a call away if I have questions," Griffin murmured.

"I may have to call you back, since I'll be working."

"How are you going to stand being away from here? You break out in a cold sweat when you have to go to Denver. Being in a big city like New York will drive you crazy."

That's exactly what worried Rory the most.

WHEN RORY WALKED INTO Rayzor Sharp Media's reception area, the first thing that hit him was how sterile the place felt. The desk was a sleek chrome-and-glass contraption with lines and angles and no warmth. A big black sign with the company name hung above it. The white walls added to the lifeless environment. He suddenly found himself missing the warm wood and earthy colors he saw everywhere at home.

A pretty little brunette dressed in black, who looked as if she hadn't eaten a decent meal in a month, glanced up and flashed him a perfect, blinding-white smile. "Hello..." She stretched out the word and looked him up and down, making him feel like a bright red apple held out to a horse. "What can I do for you?"

Man, he was out of his element. Fingering the brim of his Sunday Stetson, which he held in his hands, he said, "I'm here to see Ms. Harrington-Smyth."

"Lucky Elizabeth. Is there anything I can get you? Coffee? Bottled water? My phone number?"

For a moment he didn't know what to say. Strong women

didn't scare him, but he wanted a woman to at least give him a chance to show interest before she made an all-out play for him, and he wasn't used to being pounced on the minute he walked into a place of business.

"I'm good."

"You sure are." The receptionist pointed to a cluster of ridiculously flimsy metal chairs. "Have a seat. I'll let Elizabeth know you're here."

As he sat, he hoped the chair would hold his weight. He didn't belong here. Elizabeth's client would take one look at him, laugh and ask her if she was crazy to put this cowboy in an ad campaign to sell clothes.

Now if the client was Ford or Chevy, that he could see. Man, he wished she wanted him to sell trucks instead of jeans. That wouldn't be a bad deal. He could chuck a saddle and some grain sacks in the back of a flatbed, crawl in the cab and drive off into the sunset. Yup, that would be a sweet deal.

But he hadn't gotten that lucky.

A minute later Elizabeth walked into the reception area. She was tinier than he remembered. Heck, she couldn't be more than five-two, because she barely reached the middle of his chest, even wearing high heels. He grinned. Those spiky shoes sure made her calves look fantastic. How could such a little thing have legs that were longer than an Alaskan night?

"I'm glad you're here. I hope your flight was pleasant." She held out her hand.

He shook it, surprised at the softness of her skin. "The flight was fine."

"Thanks for getting here on such short notice. Today we're going to take some photos. I've got a meeting tomorrow with the client. You and I both work for him. Unfortunately, until we have professional shots he's unwilling to sign a contract with you or the agency."

"I can't sign the contract and have him cut me a check today?"

"Mr. Devlin insists on seeing the professional photographs first."

Rory nodded, trying to shove aside his nervousness and unease. The sooner he got to work, the sooner he'd get paid. "Then we'd best get started."

"Follow me." Elizabeth started walking. "Let me tell you a couple of things about today's shoot. We're doing this one in-house since the photos are to show the client how wonderful you'll be to showcase his jeans. When he signs the contract, we'll do the commercial and print shoots elsewhere."

She glanced at Rory as if she expected him to say something, so he replied, "Makes sense."

"I coordinate the shoot. It's my job to make sure everyone else is doing his or hers, and that we have everything we need. We've got a small set, and once you change, our photographer will take pictures of you there. But the first thing we need to do is get you into our client's designer jeans."

Designer jeans. Probably uncomfortable, tight and way too fancy. Rory followed Elizabeth down a series of hallways to a big open room, where she picked up a pair of dark blue jeans off a table.

When she held them out to him, he realized this job was going to be worse than he'd expected. Way worse.

Chapter Three

"No real man would be caught dead in these."

"Excuse me?" Elizabeth couldn't believe what Rory had just said about the client's jeans.

"I didn't mean to say that loud enough for anyone to hear."

Not an ounce of remorse showed in his clear, coffee-colored eyes, annoying her further. Her campaign rested on this cowboy, and he needed to take this job seriously. She'd fix that problem right now. "The first rule of being a spokesperson for a product, which is what we intend for you to be, is to always sing the product's praises. Never, in public or private, make any negative comments about the company, its employees or their products."

"Do I have to check with you before I say anything to anyone?"

"That might not be a bad idea until you get the hang of this business."

"I was joking."

She stared at him, not quite sure how to respond. "I know a lot of people don't value advertising, but this is a serious, competitive business."

"Lighten up. It isn't brain surgery."

Bullheaded man. Elizabeth pinched her lips together and counted to ten. If she didn't need him so desperately, she'd fire him, because obviously her words weren't hitting home.

"No, it's not brain surgery or rocket science, but that doesn't mean what we do here isn't important. We're a crucial part of the economy. If we create an ineffective campaign, company sales go down, which means people get laid off. It also means a possible fall in stock prices and less dividends for stockholders. That creates other repercussions in the economy, which I won't go into here." Mainly because Rory probably wouldn't grasp the fine nuances. "Mistakes like criticizing the company's product can cause a lot of people, you included, to lose their jobs. Are we clear on that?"

"Where do I change?"

She ignored his question for a minute, trying to determine if she'd made her point. Finally deciding the man would have to be a complete idiot not to have understood her, she pointed to a door on the opposite side of the studio. "You'll find a shirt in there. You can wear your own boots for this shoot."

While Rory changed, Elizabeth surveyed the scene around her, checking the details for the photo shoot. Micah Devlin was a perfectionist with a keen eye, and expected the same from everyone he worked with. He had to like Rory; otherwise the whole concept was a loss.

Think positively, Elizabeth. That breeds good energy, and good energy brings about good results.

The lighting was perfect. The background clean white. A saddle was propped on a hay bale, a rope casually wrapped around the saddle horn. Rats. She'd forgotten about requesting hay bales. She glanced at the set assistant. "Kudos on the set, especially on such short notice."

The young woman beamed.

Elizabeth rubbed her itching eyes. The sneezing would start soon. She dug in her purse, searching for a Claritin to stem her allergy symptoms, but came up empty. No getting around it, she'd have to suffer through.

Two more hay bales sat beside the saddle, completing the scene. Enough props to let people know Rory was a cowboy, but not enough to detract from the jeans or the cowboy. For the actual campaign she planned outdoor shots in upstate New York at a barn, on a horse, working around the place. But right now she needed to sell Rory to Devlin.

Please let him look good in the jeans.

The coffee she'd gulped an hour earlier sloshed in her nervous stomach.

Wait a minute. What was she thinking? As long as the jeans fit, he'd look terrific in them. A man that gorgeous could make anything look good. A mental picture of Rory shirtless in a pair of jeans, his chest slick as he poured water over his sweaty skin after a long day of fixing fences, flashed in her mind.

Note to self—get shots of Rory with his shirt off.

She fanned her face, though that wasn't the only place she was warm. What was she thinking? This was business. She never mixed business with pleasure, and besides that, Rory wasn't her type.

The click of stilettos on the hardwood floor interrupted Elizabeth's daydreaming. She turned to find Stephanie Jones, her black leather makeup case slung over her shoulder, sauntering toward her.

The leggy brunette stopped in front of Elizabeth. "Where's our model?"

Before she could answer, she sneezed. Not one of those polite feminine sneezes, but one with hurricane force. Darn allergies. "He's changing," Elizabeth said, after two more sneezes. "Let me explain what I'm looking for today. Just play up his natural good looks. I want him to stay real, like the cowboy he is."

"You're kidding! He's really a cowboy?" Stephanie's blue eyes sparkled as if she'd snatched up the last fifty-percent-off cashmere sweater at Barney's.

What was it about cowboys? Stephanie hadn't even seen Rory and she was drooling. Mark, the lighting tech, had about stepped on his tongue when Rory walked in.

"He's the real deal, and I want his pictures to reflect that. I want him to look like he's just stepped out of the ranch house and is heading toward the barn to work."

"In designer jeans?"

Elizabeth bristled at Stephanie's skepticism about her ad campaign.

Breathe. Don't let her negativity invade your space and make you doubt your decision. This is the right way to go with this campaign.

A big smile on her face, Elizabeth said, "Devlin Designs wants to crack the Western and middle-American market with their men's jeans."

"Okay, now using the cowboy makes sense."

"I hope the public sees it the same way. I won't keep you any longer. You need to set up, and I need to check other details of the shoot."

While the stylist traipsed across the room to the makeup table and chair, Elizabeth went to talk to Chloe.

"I can't wait to get this guy on film," she said the minute Elizabeth stopped beside her.

Just then, Rory strolled out of the dressing room. The client's designer jeans fit him perfectly, emphasizing his strong thighs. Ones he'd no doubt obtained from riding. Who'd have thought horseback riding was such a workout? But her quads and glutes had been sore for two days after her horse excursion.

Rory's tanned skin contrasted nicely with the crisp, white, snap-front, Western-style shirt she'd picked out. Denim and white. Classic, clean. One never went wrong with the basics.

She smiled at the personal touches he'd added—his belt buckle, a royal flush fanned-out poker hand, plus his boots and his cowboy hat. Rugged, but accessible.

Absolutely delicious. Absolutely perfect. Absolutely wrong for her.

"If he's any indication, they sure raise them handsome in Colorado." A sinful grin spread across Chloe's face.

Elizabeth continued staring at Rory. Before meeting him she'd have said her ideal man was more comfortable in a Brooks Brothers suit than jeans. Rory put those immaculately groomed men in their thousand-dollar suits to shame.

She started to move toward him, but Stephanie reached Rory first, introduced herself and led him to the makeup chair.

"Our model is too delectable for words," Mark said as he joined them.

This was getting a little ridiculous. "Has everyone forgotten why we're here? And no, it isn't to ogle Rory." She was beginning to think she needed to hire a bodyguard for the cowboy.

"There's no harm in looking," Mark said, glancing at him longingly.

"But with you it doesn't stop there," Chloe reminded the lighting tech.

"Plus I'm pretty sure he's heterosexual," Elizabeth added, trying to end the subject without having to give a lecture on professionalism.

"But you don't know for sure."

Elizabeth leaned toward him as if sharing a confidence. "I'm counting on you to help me out. This guy isn't a model. He doesn't understand the game. We all have to be careful that we don't scare him off. I think this might be his first visit to New York."

"All right. I'll back off. Just for you."

"I appreciate your sacrifice, Mark." She smiled in relief. "You've done a super job with the lighting, by the way. You're the best."

"Can I have that in writing for when review time rolls around?"

"Absolutely."

He glanced toward the set. "I'm off to be wonderful. I need to reposition one of the lights."

"You sure you didn't tell him to back off so you can have Rory all to yourself?" Chloe asked once Mark had left.

"Oh, please. You know my type, and Rory's not it."

"A guy doesn't have to be a Mensa candidate to be worth spending time with."

"That's the difference between us. You can be involved with someone for right now. I don't see the point in that."

"Fun and great sex." Chloe nodded toward Rory. "Look at him. I bet he's amazing in bed."

"There's more to a relationship than hot sex."

"Maybe, but that's a pretty good place to start."

"Now's not the time to talk about this," Elizabeth said, realizing how far they'd strayed off course. "Nothing can interfere with today's shoot. Be the epitome of professional."

"What he does for those jeans is amazing."

"Thank goodness."

"Not to stress you out more," Chloe said as she adjusted the height of her tripod, "but we're all counting on you to pull this one out. Word is Devlin's agency-shopping."

"This time the rumor mill's right, but I've got everything under control." Maybe if she said that enough times she'd believe it. The whole self-fulfilling prophecy thing. "Rory will help us change two crucial opinions. One, that only gay men wear designer jeans, and two, wearing designer jeans will make a man look like a pretty boy. I want the average, red-blooded, straight male to think that if a cowboy will wear these jeans, he can wear them, too."

"Then let's get this show on the road."

WITH A ROOMFUL OF PEOPLE, all with their gazes glued on his every move, Rory felt like a piece of meat. Prime choice, grade A, but meat nonetheless.

The stylist opened her black case, revealing small bottles and other containers. His stomach tightened when he recognized it was makeup. He'd figured she might have a hair dryer and hair gel in the thing. He sat horrified as she stared at him, and then selected one bottle. She dumped some of the liquid on a foam triangle and leaned toward him.

"Whoa, hold on a minute. Is that makeup?" Sissy city jeans were one thing, but no way was he wearing makeup.

The stylist nodded. The triangle moved closer.

He leaned away. "Cowboys don't wear makeup."

High-pitched giggles greeted his response. "This cowboy needs to, because if you don't wear base makeup and blush—"

Blush. Wasn't that the pink stuff women swiped over their cheeks? He resisted the urge to hang his head in shame.

"If you don't wear makeup, you'll look washed out under the lights."

"Better that than wearing that stuff. If any of my friends find out, I'll never live it down." He shuddered. "Next thing you'll be telling me I need mascara."

"It would—"

"No mascara. A man's got to draw the line somewhere."

The stylist lightly swatted his arm and giggled again. The sound grated on his nerves. "There's no need for you to worry. No one will be able to see you've got makeup on, and I swear I won't tell anyone."

Her words failed to reassure him. Something in his gut told him that his wearing makeup would get out—that was the kind of luck he had. But what choice did he have? He needed this job, and photos were the first step to landing the gig. The things he did for his mom. "I've died and gone to hell, and this is my punishment."

The woman used the sponge to dab makeup on his skin. The oily liquid slid across his face, sending ripples of revulsion through him.

"See, that's not so bad."

He gritted his teeth at the comment and refused to look in the mirror. He'd wear the blasted stuff, but no way did he want the sight of him in makeup burned into his memory.

"This doesn't detract from your masculinity at all," she declared.

He suspected she was a woman who thought a man wouldn't be interested unless she agreed with everything he said, and complimented him nonstop.

Now little Lizzie—Elizabeth, he'd decided, didn't fit her—didn't appear to let anyone tell her what to think. In an effort to tune out Stephanie's incessant chatter as she fussed with his hair, he'd watched Lizzie out of the corner of his eye.

Dressed in a black skirt and white blouse that showed off her knockout curves, she efficiently circled the room, checking lighting and the setup. What was it with all the women here wearing black? Hadn't they heard of color in New York?

As if thinking about her pulled her to him, Lizzie walked his way. "Is he ready to go, Stephanie?"

"He's perfect."

Rory almost laughed. Perfect? Not in his universe. He looked like a sissy in these tight, fancy stitched jeans. "Anybody gonna ask me if I'm ready?"

Both women turned to him, their mouths hanging open. Guess he'd broken another photo shoot protocol.

Lizzie recovered first. "I'm sorry, Rory. I didn't mean to appear rude. I need to make sure Stephanie's finished her job, which is to make sure you look your best under the lights." She turned to the stylist. "Once again, you've done super work. Now, Rory, if you'd come this way. I'd like to introduce you to the photographer before we start shooting."

Rory stood, thankful to put distance between him and Stephanie before she jumped him in the chair. "Lead on."

He liked the white shirt Lizzie had picked out for him, but the jeans wouldn't last a week on the ranch. "Just out of curiosity, how much do these pants cost?"

"The pair you're wearing retails for two hundred dollars."

He whistled. "Men actually spend their hard-earned money on these?"

"Devlin's men's jeans are among the hottest in the upscale market."

Guilt swirled inside him at the thought of playing a part in convincing people to waste money on high-priced jeans, when a pair of Wranglers or Levi's worked fine. The world was so out of whack. Kids got killed over expensive sneakers. People who couldn't pay their rent found money to get tattoos. Stuff didn't make a person. Didn't people get that?

Lizzie led him to a tall, slender woman with shoulder-length black hair, dressed in a long, flowing purple skirt and a red T-shirt with a baggy white sweater thrown over that. Big chunky beads hung around her neck. Finally, a female who wasn't dressed as if she was heading to a funeral.

She introduced herself and tossed him a look that said she was interested in more than taking his picture. What was the deal with everyone at this agency?

"Are you ready to get started?" Elizabeth asked.

"Tell me what you need me to do."

Chloe smiled. "Just be you. I'll do all the hard work. Let's start with some simple shots of you sitting here on the hay. That'll give us both a chance to warm up. I hope you don't have allergies like Elizabeth. She's been sneezing since she arrived."

"Thanks, Chloe, for pointing out the obvious." Elizabeth punctuated her statement with an unladylike sneeze, followed by a delicate "excuse me."

"The hay won't bother me. I'm around it all day long."

"Good. Chloe, you get behind the camera and see how everything looks. Rory, come with me. I'll position you."

Position him? A very intimate picture of him and Lizzie tangled together in bed popped into his head. "Excuse me?"

"I'll show you where to sit on the set, which way to look, that kind of thing. That's what we call positioning. What were you thinking?"

"I had a more intimate picture in mind." As Rory followed

her he couldn't keep his gaze off the way her little black high-heeled shoes made her hips sway, causing his blood to pump.

She froze and a pretty pink blush spread across her face. "I'm sorry you were confused."

He leaned toward her to rattle her chain a little more. After all, if he was going to be on display, he had no intention of being the only one uncomfortable. "Lizzie, if we get together, there won't be any confusion."

For a second her eyes widened and her pupils dilated. Then she swallowed hard. "My name's Elizabeth."

"You don't look like an Elizabeth. It's too long a name for such a little thing like you."

She snapped her lips together. He expected to see steam coming out her ears any minute. This job could be fun, after all.

"My parents named me Elizabeth. That's what they called me, and that's the name I go by." She crossed her arms over her chest, pulling her blouse open farther at the neck. She had a pretty neck. He'd love to kiss that spot where the vein throbbed wildly beneath her skin. "Now, if we're through with the discussion regarding my name, we both have work to do."

He smiled, way more at ease than when he'd arrived. "All set."

"Have a seat on the hay bale there." Lizzie pointed to the one closet to the saddle.

He sank onto the hay, braced his hands on his knees and leaned forward. "Now what?"

That pretty pink color still tingeing her cheeks, Lizzie turned to Chloe. "How's it look from your angle?"

"Good from here. Now, get out of the shot and let me work."

The rapid-fire click of the camera shutter filled the studio. During a momentary lull, Stephanie buzzed around him, more annoying and persistent than the horseflies at home. "I think he's getting a little shiny. Let me add some powder."

Rory tried not to wince. Just what he needed, more makeup. Pretty soon he'd look like Bozo the Clown.

She swiped a brush across his face, tossed him a big smile and fluttered away. She wasn't any better at getting the leave-me-alone signals than the horseflies.

More clicking.

This was every bit the torture he'd expected, except for the short diversion with Lizzie.

"Relax, Rory, you look like you've got a dentist appointment later today," Chloe said.

"Relax? How's a man supposed to do that with everyone staring at him, watching his every move? I feel like the turkey on Thanksgiving, sitting there in the middle of the table."

"That's an interesting point of view," Lizzie said. "It's not that everyone's watching what you do so much as ensuring nothing needs their attention."

"Try to forget everyone's here, Rory. Concentrate on one thing, and tune out everything else," Chloe suggested.

He focused on Lizzie. All straitlaced and in charge, but he'd seen a fire flash in her eyes when he'd called her that. There was definitely something there. All she needed to do was let go and channel that energy. Now that would be a job worth taking on.

"Hold that pose."

More clicking.

Lizzie leaned toward the photographer and the women whispered back and forth for a minute, before Lizzie said, "Rory, let's try some shots with you standing."

He stood, but wasn't quite sure what to do with his hands. That wasn't exactly true. Right now he'd like to have his hands on Lizzie, caressing her dynamite curves and those long legs of hers. Heat shot through him. If he didn't think about something other than her legs, these fancy jeans would get even tighter. "What do you want me to do with my hands?"

"Stand like you would if you were hanging around the ranch with friends."

When he hooked his thumbs in his front pockets, Lizzie smiled.

She seemed different when she smiled. Softer. More approachable, more womanly.

"Fabulous. Keep looking like that." The camera clicked away as Chloe rattled on. "Whatever you're thinking about, it's doing wonders for you."

Rory's gaze locked with Lizzie's. He imagined holding her, exploring her full curves. He could almost hear her excited sigh in his ears as his hands glided over her breasts and hips.

Then his phone, which he'd instinctively shoved in his back pocket, rang. Lizzie's smile evaporated, replaced with a scowl.

"Whose phone is that?" she asked. "Everyone here knows my policy on cell phones interrupting a photo shoot."

"It's mine." Rory pulled it out of his back pocket and answered the call.

He *answered* the call? Elizabeth stormed toward him. The man possessed no work ethic. "I forgot to mention that when we're at a photo shoot, everyone turns off their cell phones."

Ignoring her, he said, "I know he's trying to make it sound that way, but don't worry about it. He'll cool down."

"Get off the phone now."

"Got to go. I'll call you back later." Rory ended the call.

"I can't believe you answered that call."

"I had a life and responsibilities before this job came along. I still have things that need my attention."

"I realize that. However, I expect you to deal with those things on your own time, not on the client's." Elizabeth held out her hand.

"I'll turn it on vibrate."

"Give it to me. I'll hold on to it until we're done with the shoot." When he opened his mouth, she suspected to protest, she explained, "You can't have your phone in your back pocket. It'll ruin the line of the jeans."

Reluctantly, he handed over his BlackBerry.

"Let's get back to work." She returned to her position beside Chloe. "Where were we?"

The photographer stepped out from behind the camera. "If our focus is to sell jeans, we might want to see more of them."

"You're absolutely right, Chloe." Elizabeth tapped a manicured nail against her watch. "Got any ideas?"

"Rory, do you mind turning to the side and lifting that saddle?"

"Finally something I feel comfortable doing." He lifted the saddle and balanced the leather against his thigh, as if he'd done so every day since he was strong enough to pick it up.

Rory's gaze locked with Elizabeth's and held. Electricity shot through her. Strong. Hot. Baffling. The look in his eyes mesmerized her, making her more confident that she'd chosen the right man for the campaign.

As she watched Rory's biceps flex under his shirt, heat coursed through her. Then she glanced at his thighs. No doubt about his strength there, and his butt did amazing things for those jeans.

Oh, yeah, this shot was more than perfect.

If Micah Devlin didn't like this picture and believe the campaign would sell jeans, then there was no pleasing him.

Remembering the campaign put things back into perspective for Elizabeth. She appreciated the sight of an attractive man as much as the next woman, but this was business. She couldn't let irrational pheromones on overdrive interfere with her work.

"Angle behind him," she whispered to Chloe. No way did she want Rory hearing this conversation. "I want shots from behind."

"Butt shots coming up."

She blushed, surprised at her reaction, since she and Chloe

discussed models' body parts all the time in shoots. "We're selling jeans. The client will want to see how they look on our model from every angle."

"No need to get defensive," Chloe said as she moved to get the shots.

Elizabeth remained rooted in place, staring at Rory. The cowboy was absolutely mesmerizing. Stalwart. Confident. Any girl's best dream. Elizabeth could barely breathe. Now if Chloe could get the heat radiating from him on film...

"Rory, would you mind putting down the saddle and taking off your shirt?"

"Yes, I'd mind."

Elizabeth couldn't have heard him. Either that or he misunderstood her question. "Excuse me?"

"I don't mind putting the saddle down, but I'm not taking off my shirt."

She stood there for a moment trying to regroup.

She was in charge. She told everyone what to do and they did as requested. No one at a photo shoot questioned her decision. Not even Chloe.

This cowboy *so* pushed her buttons.

For a minute she considered ordering Rory to take off his shirt, but the glint in his eyes stopped her. He flashed her a look similar to her first boss's I'm-not-discussing-this expression. Sure, she was in charge, but her job hinged on two men's whims right now, Micah Devlin and Rory McAlister. She couldn't risk angering Rory enough that he hopped on the next plane to Colorado.

She could do this. Finesse and charm time. "Everyone take five."

The crew scooted away, though not far, in case she and Rory put on a show.

She walked to where he stood beside the hay, wanting to make their conversation as private as possible. "Rory, what's the problem?"

"There's no problem, because I'm keeping my shirt on."

She stared at him, trying to fathom what the hang-up could be. It wasn't as if she was asking him to pose for a pinup poster. Granted, she hoped this shot would have the same effect and drive women wild for him and the jeans, but they were primarily selling the product.

Maybe he was embarrassed about his chest? It couldn't be because he wasn't in shape. No way could he be hiding a beer belly under that form-fitting shirt. Okay, so what else could it be? He was a cowboy. They got thrown from horses. "Do you have some kind of injury or scar that's making this uncomfortable for you?"

"No."

"Then what's going on?"

"You told me I'd be modeling jeans, not posing for beefcake shots."

"Shots of you without your shirt will highlight the jeans, and it's what the client wants."

"We don't always get what we want."

She crossed her arms over her chest. The guy was one huge piece of granite, hard and unmoving. Needing a chance to cool off, she walked to the table with bottled water by the dressing room. She grabbed one, surprised that the top didn't pop off the way she squeezed the thing, and stormed back to Rory.

"Here, have some water." She shoved the bottle into his hands. Hopefully, the water would cool him off, too. "I need a minute."

Then she walked to the opposite side of the studio to talk to Chloe.

"I gather he's still refusing to take off his shirt?"

Elizabeth nodded. "I think he's just being stubborn."

"We've got to get the shots of him in just the jeans."

What about Rory made her want to dig in her heels? She felt as if she were six years old again, fighting with Angela Simmons. *I dare you. No, I double dare you,* and the next thing she knew, they were both sitting in Principal Mathews's office.

"You may have to pull rank." Chloe glanced toward Rory. "Look at him. How else do you think you're going to get him to cooperate?"

She followed her friend's gaze. The cowboy was leaning against the wall, his arms crossed over his strong chest. His lips formed a thin line. Nope, he hadn't let go of his anger, either.

His gaze locked with hers again. Then his chin tilted up ever so slightly and he smiled.

No way was he backing down.

She'd never been a gambler, especially when the costs were so high, and not just for her, but those who worked with her. So much rode on the campaign's success, and she needed those shots of Rory in just the jeans.

If he wanted to lock horns about this issue, he'd chosen the wrong person to mess with, because she couldn't afford to lose.

She stalked across the floor and stopped in front of Rory. She looked into his chiseled features, unmoved by his gorgeous face or his angry scowl. "I need shots of you with your shirt off. You either do as requested or you're fired."

Chapter Four

Rory, a damned good poker player, could bluff with the best of 'em, but Lizzie won this hand fair and square. Not that he would let her see how much the fact bothered him.

He unscrewed the plastic cap off his water bottle, kept his gaze focused on her and took a long drink. Then he set the bottle on the nearby table and tugged the shirttails out of his jeans. He grabbed one side in each hand and pulled. The snaps popping as they came loose broke the silence. Next, he peeled off his shirt and tossed the garment on the table.

His gaze still locked with Lizzie's, he leaned back, crossed his arms over his bare chest and said, "How's this work for you, sweetheart? Does what you see get your engine racing?"

Her cheeks immediately turned the same shade of pink as his mother's favorite roses. Lizzie blinked and swallowed.

Point to him.

"Let's get this done," he said as he walked away.

Her high heels clicked on the wood floor as she scrambled to catch up with him. "Break over, everyone."

He stopped beside the hay bales and turned toward her, deciding to have a bit more fun teasing her. "How do you want me positioned? I'm all yours."

The pulse in her neck throbbed wildly. Her eyes dilated. He smiled, knowing he'd chipped a piece out of her in-control businesswoman facade. What would Lizzie be like if she loosened up a bit? She'd be a handful who could give a man a wild ride. Now that he'd like to see.

"I'm not quite sure." After clearing her throat, she faced the photographer. "What do you think, Chloe? How should we position Rory?"

"Yes, ladies, by all means—what do you think would be my best position?"

Lizzie choked on the water she'd been about to swallow. He thumped her on the back. "You okay?"

She nodded, and he sank onto a hay bale.

"What you're doing looks amazing, Rory," Chloe said, the camera held to her eye. "Hold that pose."

As the photographer swarmed around him, clicking, his gaze never wavered from Lizzie. For all her confidence, put things on a man-woman level and she apparently didn't know what to do.

"Now cross your arms," Chloe said.

Rory started fantasizing, imagining taking Lizzie's hair out of the tight ponytail and running his fingers through the blond, curly strands. His imagination wandered further. Would the texture be as silky as he suspected? He pictured her golden hair falling around her face as she leaned over him in bed.

"Pick up the saddle." Her voice cut through his fantasy.

He stood and did as requested, but pretended he was lifting her instead. Heck, she probably weighed less than the saddle. Then an image of them flashed in his mind: of her sliding down his body and wrapping her legs around his waist. Her beautiful hair spilled down her back as she tilted her face upward, exposing her graceful neck. What kind of sounds would she make when he explored her skin with his lips?

He lowered the saddle a little to cover his rising excitement.

How long had it been since he'd had a date? Over six months. Talk about the date from hell. Their dinner conversation had consisted of her telling him all about her last boyfriend, who she'd dated for five years, and how he'd dumped her. Rory's previous relationship had been over a year ago, and since he wasn't a casual sex kind of guy, that was the last time he'd been intimate.

He stared long and hard at Lizzie. Something about her reached out to him. Danged if he knew what, because a lot of women were prettier.

"Stephanie, mist Rory." Lizzie tossed the request over her shoulder. "I want him to look like he's been working up a sweat."

Confidence. She had an air about her. Maybe that was what appealed to him. Such a tiny woman and yet she looked as if she'd stand up to a grizzly. Had to be either her assurance or his dry spell that accounted for his body's unusual reaction.

The stylist popped up in front of him with a water bottle. The moisture sprayed on his chest instantly reminded him that he stood half-naked in front of a group of people, and that Lizzie had threatened to fire him unless he agreed to comply. His daydreams burned like dry kindling tossed on a campfire.

"You're doing a fantastic job." Stephanie batted her long eyelashes. "Once this campaign hits the street, Devlin jeans are going to fly off the shelf."

He didn't care whether or not the jeans sold well. All that mattered was that he earned thirty grand. Then he'd kiss this big city and modeling goodbye.

"Rory, set down the saddle and put on your hat," Chloe said.

Bossy city women. *Rory, do this. Rory, turn and look at me. Rory, you need to focus.* He felt like an elementary schoolkid having a bad day.

"Push your hat back a little. We need to see more of your face." This order came from Lizzie. "Cross your arms over your chest," she called out next.

Good thing, because he was about to put his hands around her pretty little throat.

"I think we have everything we need," she finally said. "Let's call it a day, everyone."

He walked past her to where he'd left his shirt, slipped the garment on and returned to her. He leaned down, not wanting anyone to overhear. "Next time we have a disagreement—" and based on today's events, future disagreements were a sure thing "—we work them out in private. Don't ever pull rank on me again. I don't perform on command."

"Neither do I," she called out to his back.

Damned if the little minx wasn't a spitfire, and damned if he didn't admire her for that.

RORY'S WORDS HAMMERED in Elizabeth's head as she walked to her office. How dare he speak to her like that? Then to top things off, he'd walked away without allowing her to say anything but the lamest of comebacks.

She'd definitely needed to set ground rules with the cowboy. He wasn't in Colorado anymore, and the New York business world ran differently than a horse ranch. His open defiance of her authority had to stop. Otherwise, they'd butt heads constantly and make everyone miserable. An uncomfortable environment bred negativity, which led to poor work performance and an unhappy client.

When she arrived in her office, she found Chloe at her desk, downloading photos. Her friend glanced upward. "I don't know how you work in this office. It's too ordered. Doesn't that stifle your creativity?"

"An orderly work space leads to an orderly mind." Her grandmother's pet phrase popped out before Elizabeth could stop it. She slid the chair from in front of her desk to the other side, close to the computer, and threw herself into the seat. "Sleep deprivation's warping my mind, and turning me into my grandmother."

"It could be worse."

"How?"

Chloe shrugged. "I'm not sure. That just sounded like the

thing to say. Wait a minute, I've got it. The good news is getting sleep will fix the problem."

"I wish that would work on my problem with Rory. I hope he's not going to continue to be so difficult."

"What was with you two, anyway?" Chloe asked. "Playing referee is not in my job description, and if it's going to be in the future, I want more money."

"He pushed every one of my buttons today. The man could write a book on how to become the world's biggest pain in the ass."

"Apparently the sparks are still flying."

"Can you believe he refused to take off his shirt? I don't get what the big deal was. It wasn't like I was asking him to pose in his underwear."

"If I could figure guys out, do you think I'd be here?" Chloe pulled up the first set of photos onto the computer screen, the ones of Rory sitting on the hay bale. "No, I wouldn't. I'd be in the Caribbean living off the money I made from my *New York Times* bestseller on how to understand men."

"Wouldn't that be nice?"

Chloe pointed to the monitor. "Check these out."

Elizabeth stared at the photos. Rory had a presence. Incredible, steamy, make-a-woman's-insides-tingle-with-a-look presence. "The shots are fantastic, but they don't showcase the jeans."

"I agree, but do you want to put one of these in a portfolio to show Devlin how well Rory photographs?"

"Couldn't hurt."

Chloe clicked computer keys and a second later the printer hummed to life. "Now, about you and Rory, I wasn't talking about the arguing type of sparks. I was talking about the making-you-all-hot-and-bothered ones."

Elizabeth stood and retrieved the photo from the printer. "I don't know what you mean."

Good comeback. That'll make her drop the subject.

She laughed. "You never were a good liar."

"So, I admit it. The guy drives me crazy."

Chloe flashed her an annoying best-friend, know-it-all smile.

"I didn't mean that in a good way," Elizabeth stated. "He's stubborn, inflexible, and refuses to take directions or criticism well."

"One person's fighting is another person's dancing."

"That's the silliest thing I've ever heard." After tossing the photo onto the desk blotter, Elizabeth sank back into her chair. "If you're trying to say I enjoyed arguing with him today, you're way off base."

"You may not have had fun, but he was having a blast seeing your temper flare. Think about what it would be like making up with him. Oooh!"

"You think Rory was being difficult on purpose? Why would he do that?"

Chloe shrugged and pulled up more photos on the computer screen. These of Rory holding the saddle.

"If he was, he has a sick sense of humor," Elizabeth declared. "A man with self-respect and a decent work ethic wouldn't enjoy making his boss uncomfortable." She tapped the monitor. "Print out that one."

Chloe nodded. "Think about it from his point of view. He's a strong, assertive man, a lone cowboy. I'm guessing Rory doesn't take orders from too many people."

"Then he's going to have to start learning who's at the top of the food chain."

"When Devlin signs the contract and you center the jeans campaign on Rory, you're going to have to find a way to co-exist."

"It'll be easy. I plan for this campaign to do major things for my career." That is, if Rory didn't drive her completely insane first. Elizabeth paced the length of her office, stopping at her credenza to straighten the silver Effie Award she'd received for the Tug-Ups training pants ad she'd created last year.

Courage and self-esteem bolstered, she reasoned she could work with Rory. After all, she worked with Micah Devlin.

"Saving the Devlin account and creating a nationwide campaign can turn management supervisors into vice presidents. When Rory's driving me insane, I'll visualize my new, spacious, vice-presidential office."

"Ah, yes. Your ten-year plan."

Elizabeth ignored her friend's sarcasm. Chloe wasn't a big believer in planning, preferring to remain open to life's opportunities because goals stifled her. Elizabeth believed that to achieve what she wanted took goal setting, strategic planning and a lot of visualization.

Chloe leaned forward in her chair and whistled. "Look at these photos. Cowboy here just might take both our careers places."

Elizabeth gazed at the pictures. Rory stared back at her, his boots firmly planted on the ground, the white shirt pulled taut across his pecs, his biceps bulging as he held the saddle. The man would become the stuff women dreamed of. "Print that one."

Chloe nodded, and scrolled through more photos. A few seconds later, she clicked on an image to enlarge it, then leaned back in her chair and sighed dreamily. "One of the perks of my job, butt shots of gorgeous men." She tapped the computer screen with her dark purple nail. "And that man has one fine butt."

Glancing at the photo, Elizabeth kept her lips pinned together for fear she'd start drooling. Once she had her emotions well under control, she said, "Remember the focus of our campaign is the jeans, not on how good the model's butt is."

"Are you saying you disagree with my assessment?"

She'd have to be blind to disagree. Not that she'd admit the fact to Chloe, for fear of eternal taunting. "My job is to focus on how the jeans look."

"Which is pretty damn good on his butt."

"Print the first one and the shot where he's looking over his shoulder at us."

"You mean the one where he looks like he's ready to carry you off into the sunset?"

"If that's the third shot, then yes. We'll add that to the portfolio." Elizabeth stared at the photo. Rory's eyes had darkened to a deep walnut color, and he had the slightest smile on his face. "What makes you say he was thinking of me? Maybe he was thinking about you."

"Don't I wish." Chloe sighed again. "But alas, his gaze followed you around the room."

That information should've made Elizabeth warm in all kinds of places, but instead the fact worried her. She couldn't afford having Rory see her as anything but his boss. "He can't be interested in me. Can he?"

"Why's that so unbelievable?"

"We're ill-suited."

"Opposites attract."

"You're full of clichés today."

"You're just ticked because I'm right, and don't try to change the subject. It's true. Opposites do attract."

"They may have instant chemistry, but those relationships don't last. The ones that do are based on things like similar values and interests." Needing something to busy her hands and control her nervousness, Elizabeth grabbed a pen and fiddled with it. "Pull up the shots of him shirtless."

"You'd give a guy up because you worked together? Even if you thought he was your soul mate?"

"There's no such thing. In a world of over six billion people, there has to be more than one man I could have a lasting relationship with."

Chloe shook her head. "If I thought a guy was the one, I wouldn't let anything get in the way."

The last shots of Rory popped onto the screen. Chloe whistled through her teeth. "Be still my heart. These are the best yet. Look at those six-pack abs."

Elizabeth stared at the photo, speechless. Rory could make a nun think twice about her vow of chastity. Hell, think three times about it. "Make that one poster-size. I'll put it on an easel. Put the rest in a portfolio. I'm off to make sure the mock-ups are ready for tomorrow."

Pointing at the picture displayed on the computer monitor, Chloe said, "That's all you've got to say about this?"

"I think it's excellent. It should accomplish exactly what we need it to."

Her friend flopped back in her chair and threw her hands in the air. "And that's why you don't date much."

"Can we stick to the job here, and stay off the topic of my love life?"

"What love life?"

Elizabeth pointedly ignored her jibe, mainly because she lacked a good comeback. Tough to argue with the truth.

Her dating had been a little sparse lately, but that was because she had standards. If she let her friends set her up she could have three dates a week, but what was the point of dating if the candidates fell below par? On top of that, her job's long hours left little time for a social life. But more importantly, she had no intention of letting dating sidetrack her from what mattered—saving Devlin's accounts and advancing her career. That required work and sacrifice. Everything worthwhile did.

"How can looking at this gorgeous guy, one you'll be working in close contact with, not make your body sing?"

"I'm tone-deaf."

Listening to her body, being ruled by her hormones, led down a scary path. Going against common sense led to caring, wanting, expectations and possibly loving. All of those things, in her experience, led to heartbreak. No, thanks. Been there, done that. Gave away the T-shirt.

"I don't have time for anything except getting ready for tomorrow's meeting." Elizabeth glanced at her watch. Eight o'clock. The night was zooming by at warp speed. "I still have to come up with a slogan before the morning meeting."

"Got any ideas?"

"I have a bunch written down, but now that we've got Rory's pictures they don't seem right." She rubbed her throbbing temples. "I want something memorable, like the Calvin Klein ad with Brooke Shields. 'Nothing gets between me and my Calvins.'"

"Think about Rory's qualities."

"He's stubborn to the point of pigheadedness."

"His good qualities."

She thought for a minute. "He's strong. He's authentic."

"He sure is a real man, and very delectable."

Rory's comment that no real man would wear designer jeans popped into Elizabeth's head. She grabbed a Post-it note and scribbled out a line as adrenaline gushed through her system, invigorating her. "I've got the slogan, Chloe, and it's perfect."

BY THE MORNING MEETING in the agency's conference room, Elizabeth was running on stress and caffeine. The stuff that fueled corporate America. Once she presented a hopefully coherent campaign to Micah Devlin and answered his questions, which if past meetings were any indication would be many, she planned on collapsing and sleeping for two days straight.

When she escorted Devlin, dressed in a pair of his own jeans and a pin-striped button-down shirt, into the conference room, he sat at the long mahogany table and pulled out his iPad.

She smoothed the skirt of her charcoal-gray Ellen Tracy suit and glanced down at her red stiletto pumps. Chloe called them her ruby slippers, because Elizabeth felt invincible when she wore then.

Ruby slippers, do your magic. "We believe Rory McAlister is the perfect person to represent Devlin Designs' men's jeans."

Elizabeth pulled the cover off the poster on the easel, revealing Rory—naked from the waist up, his arms crossed over his wide chest, his biceps bulging, his skin slick with sweat—wearing the company's jeans and his cowboy hat. Below the picture ran the words *Devlin men's jeans. Strong enough to stand up to a real man.*

Her breath stuck in her throat as she waited for her client to respond. When she'd first met Micah Devlin she'd been attracted to him. In his mid to late thirties, he was approximately five or so years older than her, and she liked that. He had an MBA from Harvard Business School. Was the CEO of the family business—a Fortune 500 company, no less. He was tall, in shape without being overly muscular. His company contributed to numerous charities. He'd seemed like her dream man. At least on paper.

Then she'd gotten to know him. His controlling personality and micromanaging had effectively incinerated her attraction.

No worries about mixing business and pleasure there.

"I like him," Devlin said. "He's strong and fit, but doesn't look like he spends all day in the gym."

Relief burst through her, making her knees weak, but Elizabeth clamped down on the emotion. There would be time to celebrate later, once the contracts were signed, her agency's with Devlin and his with Rory.

"That's exactly what we were trying to portray. His strength comes from working with his hands and his back, like so many Americans."

"Do you plan to weave that hardworking attitude into the campaign?"

"Definitely."

Devlin jotted down notes on the iPad. "What're the rest of your plans?"

"I thought we'd start with the Times Square billboard, since Devlin Designs has it booked for the next three months. We'd pair that with ads in the *New York Times,* the *Chicago Tribune* and *USA Today.*"

"I understand the newspapers' appeal, but I'm not so certain about the billboard. Sure, it'll be seen by millions of tourists, but other than that, how will it help us appeal to middle America?"

His question momentarily threw her off stride. Her grandmother's voice rang in her head. *Is that really the decision you want to make? Have you thought this through thoroughly, Elizabeth?*

Shaking herself mentally, she tuned out her grandmother. Elizabeth refused to be intimidated, when she'd prepared for this meeting until three in the morning, and this was one of the questions she'd anticipated. "I think showcasing Rory on June's billboard is the quickest way to create a buzz while we're finalizing magazine ads and shooting the TV commercial. When people see Rory's picture, they'll want to know who he is. Women will hit your website en masse to find out more about him. We'll add a new page to the site—meet Devlin Designs' newest model. We'll get him tweeting, to add to the buzz. That excitement should help me book spots for him on the morning show circuit."

Devlin tapped his pen on the table. "Plus the billboard should give us a boost to our East Coast sales."

Elizabeth nodded, the knot between her shoulder blades loosening. What was it about Devlin that cracked her self-confidence? "The average man is going to want to look like Rory. Women will think if their man wears your jeans he'll look like Rory. The gay man is going to want to date him. No matter what, they're going to check out Devlin jeans. I think we'll get an excellent return on the investment. Even though we're targeting a different market, everything fashionwise starts here in New York."

"Since we can't use the ad we'd planned on for the May billboard because of that model's scandal, let's showcase the jeans and introduce Rory instead."

Elizabeth stared at Devlin, momentarily stunned. A billboard took a minimum of two weeks to put together, and today was April 16.

What did this guy think? That she twitched her nose like Samantha on *Bewitched,* and billboards magically appeared?

"If we go with this shot—" Elizabeth pointed to the easel and Rory's gorgeous beefcake photo "—we might be able to pull it off."

"I like it. An outdoor scene on a billboard will clutter up the message anyway. I don't want anything distracting from the cowboy, the slogan and the company name." Devlin clicked his pen as he thought. "Do what you have to, within reason, to get the job done. If you think the budget needs to be revised, let me know."

Elizabeth nodded. So much for sleeping for two days after this meeting.

"What's this cowboy's voice like?" Devlin asked. "Can he do the commercial work or will we need to hire a voice-over actor?"

"Rory has a pleasant voice with a slight Western drawl, which will work perfectly for the campaign."

"Pleasant? We need more than that for our spokesman."

"Forgive me. That was a poor choice of words. His voice is hardly average." She couldn't tell this Fortune 500 CEO that Rory's voice sent ripples of excitement through her and made her lace panties damp. Or could she? "The women at the shoot commented that his voice was as good as his looks."

"I've got a lot riding on this. Before I sign this cowboy and the agency contract I want to know what he sounds like."

Warning bells clanged in Elizabeth's head. Considering

Rory's unpredictable behavior at the photo shoot, the thought of him meeting Devlin sent dread snaking down her spine. She counted to ten.

Never let a client see uncertainty. It's the kiss of death.

She smiled at Devlin. "Do you want to meet him in person or would a demo CD work?"

Please say the latter.

Devlin had been about to answer her when his cell phone played "I Could've Danced All Night." He grabbed it out of his briefcase. "Excuse me. I have to take this."

Phone to his ear, he stepped outside the conference room.

She couldn't believe that Micah Devlin, who chastised her when she took a call from another client with an "emergency," had answered his phone. Obviously, he subscribed to the do-as-I-say, not-as-I-do philosophy.

"What's up?" his surprisingly gentle voice floated in through the open door. "Can it wait? My day is full of meetings."

While Elizabeth longed to scoot her chair to where she could actually see him as he talked on the phone, she resisted the urge. Innocently overhearing a conversation and openly eavesdropping were two different things, and she had no desire to be caught doing the latter.

"Don't do that," Devlin almost pleaded. "You know the doctor told you not to drive for three weeks. Please wait." Frustration crept into his voice. "I'll run by the pharmacy after this meeting. I'll be there in a half an hour tops." Again he paused. "I love you, too, Nana."

Elizabeth hoped she'd concealed her shock when he returned to the conference table, phone in hand, the softness she'd heard in his voice only seconds ago nowhere visible in his eyes. Who would've thought he actually had relatives, much less one he cared about?

"Since Rory McAlister will be a company spokesperson,

I want to talk to him face-to-face. I need to make sure he can have a coherent conversation."

Elizabeth swallowed hard. Sure she knew Rory's voice sent a women's happy hormones into overdrive, but how would he do when a reporter tossed questions at him? How could she have forgotten that when she'd developed the campaign? Details mattered, especially to Devlin.

"I met Rory on a ranch in Colorado. He's used to interacting with tourists. He was quite engaging with facts and local-color tidbits." At least he'd appeared to be, from the bits and pieces of stories she'd heard, riding at the end of the line of horses.

"He'd better be able to handle interviews."

"I assure you he will." Elizabeth smiled. By his first interview she'd be certain he was prepared. She could make a fortune in Vegas playing high stakes poker with her bluffing skills.

"Once I've talked with this cowboy and am convinced he'll suit our needs, I'll sign him to a contract. Then I'll sign the jeans contract with your agency. Set up the meeting for tomorrow."

She noted he hadn't mentioned renewing the other lines' contracts. He probably still wanted that leverage to hold over her.

Devlin pulled his iPhone out of his pocket and punched a couple of buttons. "Ten works for me. I don't want to see his face everywhere, by the way. When the public sees him, I want them to think of Devlin Designs."

"I agree. I suggest you have your legal department add an exclusivity clause to the standard contract."

"You don't think his agent will balk?"

"He's currently representing himself."

Devlin smiled openly for the first time. "Then there's no need to pay him thirty grand over the course of this campaign. What do you think we can get him for?"

Sleep deprivation had to be playing tricks with her hearing, or had rotted her brain cells, because they'd extensively discussed what to pay a spokesman, even an unknown, before she'd started her search. "I told Rory he'd make thirty thousand, as per our discussions."

Devlin picked a piece of lint off his spotless shirt. "When we talked, we discussed a lot of options, from models to rodeo cowboys. That amount seems a little steep for an unknown with no experience."

Elizabeth swas seated and folded her hands in front of her to keep from shaking the man silly. Glancing into his eyes, she realized the truth. He'd changed his mind about the money when he'd discovered Rory lacked an agent.

"Offer him twenty thousand," Devlin stated.

"This puts me in an awkward position. Rory and I had a verbal agreement."

Devlin folded his arms across his chest. His sharp gaze bore through her. "I pay your agency to negotiate with models on my behalf."

What was it lately, with men drawing a line in the sand with her? "I'll inform Rory of your wishes, and will do everything in my power to get him to agree to the new terms."

"Make sure you've dealt with the money issue by the time we meet tomorrow."

"I'd feel more comfortable taking a day or two to prepare before I discuss the subject with Rory."

"I want him signed to a contract so we can move forward with this campaign." Devlin's icy tone and granite gaze left no room for further discussion.

"I'll talk to him today."

Chapter Five

Elizabeth walked down the hallway to Chloe's office and suppressed the urge to bang her head against the wall.

"Shoot me now and put me out of my misery. I've lost the will to live," she said as she sank into the wooden chair in front of her friend's desk. Now that the adrenaline and caffeine had worn off, exhaustion claimed her.

Chloe paled. "Do I need to update my résumé for the next round of layoffs?"

"No, but you might want to measure me for a straitjacket, because I'm going to lose my mind working with Devlin."

"What happened?"

"I have two new problems. The first being Devlin wants to meet with Rory before he'll sign the contract."

"Why is that a problem? Rory's perfect."

"He's a cowboy, and his mystical cowboy charm won't work on Micah Devlin."

"Rory will do fine."

"I'm not so sure. When I first gave him the jeans for the shoot, he said no real man would be caught dead in them. Can you believe that?"

"Since you're still talking about Rory in the present tense, I assume you didn't kill him. But what did you do after he said that?"

She glared at her friend. "I'm not the Wicked Witch of the East, you know."

"I didn't say you were. It's just you get a little overzealous sometimes, especially when people make mistakes in their job."

"I very calmly and professionally pointed out the important points of being a company spokesperson."

"I bet that went over like a lead balloon. Guys love having a woman tell them they screwed up."

"I think he took it well, but after the jeans comment, you can see why I'm concerned about him talking with Devlin. All I need is for Rory to say something negative about the product."

"He won't, since you set him straight."

"You're just saying that because he's good-looking. In an interview situation, he'll have to think on his feet, and who knows what someone might ask him? What if he doesn't stop to think before he answers, and blurts out the first thing that pops into his head?" Once Elizabeth started voicing her concerns, she couldn't hold them back. "Sure, he's photogenic, but I have no idea what kind of education Rory has, or whether he can hold an intelligent conversation. What if he can't talk about anything but horses, mucking out a stall and fixing fences?"

"Whoa. Can we slow down this runaway train? Rory doesn't need to be a Rhodes scholar to do well on the morning show circuit. He's got a great personality and charisma. Those two things can't be taught, and will go a long way in an interview. Plus you'll prep him."

When Elizabeth opened her mouth to speak, Chloe held up her hand. "If you're worried about anything else, talk to Rory. Find out about his education and background. Ask him how he feels about doing interviews."

"Men have such fragile egos. What if he hasn't graduated high school, and my asking about his education embarrasses him? There has to be a reason he's a cowboy and not a white-collar businessman. He might get mad enough to quit."

"How much sleep have you gotten this week?"

"Not much."

"You must be dead-tired, Elizabeth. This kind of situation never flusters you. In fact, you thrive on a challenge."

"I'm beginning to understand why sleep deprivation is so effective in breaking down prisoners of war." Elizabeth walked to the small refrigerator in the corner of Chloe's office, pulled out a can of Red Bull, popped the top open and took a long drink. Within seconds the caffeine bolted through her system, reviving her brain cells. "You're right. I can do this. I can use Rory's male ego to my advantage. I'll tell him I need his opinion on Devlin's concerns and the rest of the campaign."

"Guys like that. They're fixers."

"While we're talking, I can identify any weaknesses he might have in a business meeting or an interview situation."

"Good, problem number one under control. What's the second problem?"

Elizabeth squeezed the Red Bull can. The sound of crumpling aluminum filled the room. "Devlin has decided the money I quoted Rory, the price we discussed at length beforehand, is too much to pay. He wants me to renegotiate the deal."

Chloe leaned back in her chair and threw her hands in the air. "You're going down in flames."

"What happened to playing the encouraging best friend and colleague?"

"Sorry, I can't lie that well. No way is Rory going to take your news well. Not that I blame him. If someone quoted me one amount for a job, and then wanted to low-ball me, I'd throw a fit, too."

"That's what I'm afraid of." Elizabeth resisted the urge to pick at her nail polish. "Devlin wants me to have renegotiated Rory's contract by tomorrow's meeting."

"Push the meeting back."

"I tried. Devlin refused."

"Sure sucks to be you."

Elizabeth grabbed a scrap of paper off the desk, wadded it up and tossed it at her friend. The shot fell short, landing in Chloe's lap. "I don't need you pointing out the obvious. What I need are suggestions on how to keep Rory from strangling me when I talk to him."

"The best you can hope for is avoiding a major scene and/or violence."

Elizabeth laid her head on the desk. "You're right. I'm going down in flames." She peeked up at Chloe. "Where did you go the last time you were going to break up with a guy and you were worried he'd make a scene?"

"I'll chalk up that comment as a stress-induced insensitivity." Chloe tossed the wad of paper at Elizabeth, and it bounced off her head. "When I was worried Jason would make a scene when I broke up with him, I did the deed at Bar American."

"Brilliant idea." Elizabeth straightened. "Hope springs eternal. No one makes a scene at a restaurant, especially one of Bobby Flay's."

"That idea will cost two white peach margaritas from Mesa Grill."

"Well worth the price, and speaking of Mesa Grill, I think we'll eat there. The Southwestern food and atmosphere are more Rory's style." Elizabeth stood and walked across the room. "I'm off to call him. Hopefully he hasn't eaten yet. I've got the making-a-scene issue under control, but how am I going to convince him to take a pay cut?"

"I have no idea. You're on your own there."

"That's what I'm afraid of."

As she walked out of Chloe's office, she told herself to think positive and pray, because that was her only hope—divine intervention.

ELIZABETH ARRIVED at the restaurant fifteen minutes early, in the hopes that by the time Rory showed up she'd have developed a strategy to convince him to agree to the pay reduction. As she waited, she told herself she wasn't doing anything wrong. Rory hadn't been signed to a contract. She acted on behalf of the client with the model. Despite all those logical reasons, the thought of renegotiating his contract left her feeling a little sleazy.

She'd think positive. Would convince him this setback wasn't permanent. He could turn this into an opportunity to impress the client, and get a huge raise on the next contract.

Elizabeth thought for a minute. How lame was that? Unless Rory was comatose, no way would he buy it.

She glanced around the restaurant. Hanging on one wall was a picture of a cow. Another had a picture of John Wayne in classic cowboy pose and dress. The booth upholstery was a print of cowboys on horses. Rory would fit right in. The restaurant should remind him of hearth and home, and hopefully put him in a good mood.

By the time he arrived, ten minutes late, she hadn't come up with a better option. After the maître d' showed him to the table, Elizabeth bit her lip and resisted the urge to lecture him about the importance of promptness for business meetings.

His hair was damp, as if he'd just crawled out of the shower, and curled at the collar of his plain white shirt. With that he wore a pair of navy slacks. She smiled when she noticed he still had on his cowboy boots and the royal flush belt buckle. Cowboy *GQ*. Not bad. Her pulse jumped. Seeing him now made her realize what a fool Devlin was to risk losing Rory by haggling over money.

"I appreciate you meeting with me after such a long day." She looked pointedly at her watch once he sat across from her.

"I had to eat. This way you're picking up the tab."

Elizabeth winced. If Rory was worrying about the cost of

dinner, Chloe was right. She would go down in flames once she brought up renegotiating his salary.

For a moment she focused on the menu, not quite sure where to begin. Business meetings usually never bothered her, so why was this one making her uncomfortable? And it was more than the fact that she had to renegotiate his contract. Maybe because across the table from her sat one gorgeous man. She scoffed at the idea. She'd been alone at similar meetings before with way better-looking male models.

Gay models. Big deal.

From the red-hot glance he'd tossed her when he'd pulled off his shirt this afternoon, the man had to be straight. No gay man could look a woman in the eyes like that and nearly singe her eyebrows.

The waiter took their drink orders, pulling her away from her unsettling thoughts. Deciding her brain was fuddled enough from lack of sleep, and this was a business meeting, she stuck with water. Rory ordered a beer.

To repair any damage she'd done to their karma that afternoon, Elizabeth said, "First of all, I wanted to apologize if I offended you in any way at the shoot today. I'm afraid I may have come off a little harsh. There's so much riding on this campaign, and it's put me a bit on edge."

"I'm a big boy. I can take it."

His words, coupled with his sultry gaze, sent tremors rippling through Elizabeth. She grabbed her water glass and took a long sip, not quite sure what to make of his comment. The man either loved playing word games or was clueless about how what he said sounded to other people.

Since ignoring the comment provided the wisest course, Elizabeth barreled onward. "I wanted to apprise you of what transpired today in my meeting with Micah Devlin." Start with the positives. She sucked in a deep breath and smiled. "He was very happy with your photos. He thinks you definitely have the image and the presence he's looking for to represent his company's jeans."

Rory nodded, grabbed a slice of sourdough bread and slathered it with butter. "What's our next step?"

Out of the corner of her eye Elizabeth noticed an attractive redhead with perfect teeth flashing a smile Rory's way.

"We hope to get you on some morning shows."

He nodded again, revealing no signs of panic in his voice or his facial expression. Good. Elizabeth relaxed her grip on her water glass.

The redhead continued to stare. A stunning blonde at the bar looked at Rory as if she wanted to skip dinner and go straight to him for dessert.

On the good-news side, he garnered exactly the reaction Elizabeth had hoped for with women. On the negative side, having them openly drooling over him set off a feeling alarmingly close to jealousy in her.

"How do you feel about doing interviews?" she asked. "Have you had any experience with that kind of situation?"

"I've been interviewed for the local paper a time or two."

"Good." That was better than nothing. Barely. "Then you're used to having a reporter ask you questions." Elizabeth almost stumbled over her words. What kind of tough questions could a local reporter ask? *What do you think of the price of grain at the feed store?* "Sometimes a reporter will put you on the spot. If you think it'll make you more comfortable, we could do some practice interviews."

"Whatever you say."

Why was he being so agreeable? Nervousness tickled her spine. This couldn't be the same man who'd refused to take off his shirt earlier today. Something was up, and from her interactions with Rory so far, she reasoned it couldn't be good. Either that or the man had undergone a stubbornectomy since their photo shoot.

She shook herself mentally. Quit borrowing trouble.

The waiter placed a glass in front of Rory, then poured the bottled beer and asked if he could take their orders.

"The ancho chile-honey glazed salmon is superb. I highly recommend it." She turned to the waiter. "In fact, that's what I'll have tonight."

He nodded and turned to Rory.

"I'll have the rib eye, rare, and a side of mashed potatoes."

It figured he was a meat-and-potatoes guy. She took a drink of water and focused on her goal.

"Back to the interviews," Elizabeth said, once the waiter departed. "When I met you in Colorado, you seemed fairly comfortable talking to people."

"I hold my own."

"On the guided tours you talk about your local community and its history. Are you comfortable talking about other things?"

His right eyebrow inched upward. "I'm aware of what's going on in the world. We get cable and everything in Estes Park."

She mentally cringed. How did she keep managing to say the wrong thing? She'd never been prone to that before. "I didn't mean to imply you didn't. I was wondering what topics you felt comfortable talking about in an interview."

"I can talk about most anything. Being in the tourist industry has taught me to think on my feet. You wouldn't believe some of the situations that come up." Then he smiled. She almost reached into her purse for her sunglasses. "Or maybe you would, considering our first meeting."

Her mouth went dry. His smile could make Mother Teresa sin. Elizabeth had to get that smile on film.

"The main thing to remember in interviews is to be upbeat and personable."

"And to be positive about the client's product. See, I can be taught."

She laughed. The man possessed quite a sense of humor. "I

forget that this is all new to you, and you're not a professional model. I also proposed television commercials to Devlin as part of the campaign. He wants to meet you before we go further. He's a bit of a control freak."

"Takes one to know one."

She bristled until she looked at him. Humor shone in his sparkling brown eyes. "I could say the same for you."

"Sure could. That's what made today's photo session hard for me. Seemed like everyone was telling me what to do. I'm not used to that."

She made a mental note to slow down and explain things to him on future shoots.

"FYI, the only one you need to listen to is me, unless the client's present."

"I'll keep that in mind."

She liked this easygoing man a lot better than the pain-in-the-ass model from earlier in the day. Too bad she had to spoil things by bringing up salary issues.

"Devlin wants to meet you tomorrow at ten. Will that work for you?"

"I'm at your service."

Rory's slow drawl wrapped around her, sending a rush of heat through her system. If he used that voice in TV commercials, women would cause a stampede on their way to department stores to buy Devlin's men's jeans.

"I appreciate your flexibility," she said as their waiter placed their entrées in front of them.

The redhead who'd been eyeing Rory since he arrived, now finished with her meal, sauntered toward their table on a roundabout way to the front door. All the while she eyed Rory like an air force pilot preparing for a precision strike. She slowed down beside their table and then "accidentally" dropped her purse right at Rory's feet.

He reached down, picked up the woman's crimson leather bag and held it out to her. When she accepted it, she none too subtly slipped a piece of paper into his hand, smiled and strutted away.

How could she hit on a guy when he was with another woman? Elizabeth was amazed at such tackiness. She stared at Rory and waited. What straight man under the age of eighty wouldn't take this gorgeous woman up on what she so obviously offered?

He tossed the paper on his bread plate without even glancing at the note.

Wonders never ceased. Elizabeth scooped up a piece of salmon. Knowing her time was running out, she found the expertly cooked fish tasted like paper in her mouth. She needed to get to the money issue before they finished their entrées. "Is there anything you're concerned about with our meeting tomorrow with Devlin?"

"Should I be?"

No, I'm the one who should be worried, since Devlin wanted me to renegotiate your salary.

She shook her head. "Devlin wants to meet you before he officially puts his stamp of approval on the campaign and signs the contracts, but we shouldn't have any problems. You're the right person for the job."

She knew she should bring up the subject of money, but couldn't. The topic change would bring their pleasant dinner to a quick and deadly end. "How long have you lived in Colorado?"

"All my life. I'm third-generation. All my family's there."

She couldn't imagine living where her parents and grandparents lived. Probably because her parents never stayed very long in one place.

"How 'bout you?"

"I've lived in New York state all my life, but I've only lived here in the city since I graduated from college."

She paused, hoping he would share his educational background with her. When he didn't, she gathered it was probably because he lacked a college education.

When the waiter cleared away their dinner plates, Elizabeth knew she couldn't avoid the salary issue any longer. She took a long drink of water and then forced the words past her tight throat before she chickened out. "There was one thing Devlin wanted me to discuss with you before tomorrow's meeting." She swallowed hard, struggling to choose the correct words. Hell, there weren't words that would make this any easier. "Seeing as you have no name recognition and no experience—"

"You said that made me interesting."

He remembered that, huh? Figured. He possessed the most inconvenient memory. "Name recognition and experience are vital in the modeling industry, and factor into what a company is willing to pay. Because you lack those two things Mr. Devlin feels thirty thousand for the campaign is a little high. He thinks twenty thousand is more reasonable."

There. She'd gotten the words out. She waited for the hurricane to hit.

"We agreed to thirty thousand," Rory said, his voice low and unexpectedly calm, like the air before the storm hit and tossed trees and buildings around.

"Yes, that's what we discussed, but we haven't signed a contract."

She considered telling Rory to get an agent to watch out for his best interest, but her conscience balked at the idea. She and Rory worked for Devlin Designs. In this situation she represented her agency and her client, not the model.

Rory crossed his arms over his chest. His gaze drilled into her. "I can head right on back to Colorado. My job there's waiting for me. It's no skin off my nose."

Chapter Six

After delivering his ultimatum, Rory took a long swallow of beer, hoping the icy liquid would calm his rising temper. He should've known better than to trust Lizzie. Obviously, he hadn't learned the don't-trust-career-driven-city-women lesson well enough from Melissa.

Memories rushed back. They'd met at Harvard, and he, young idealistic fool that he'd been, had fallen madly in love. They'd made plans for a future together, or least he thought they had.

He'd believed Melissa loved him enough to follow him to Colorado. When she accepted his proposal she'd agreed to live with him on the ranch, but the closer the wedding date loomed on the calendar, the more she waffled, until she finally admitted she'd changed her mind. She wanted him to move to Boston instead, and if he wouldn't the engagement was off.

Now here he sat across the table from another bossy city woman, and apparently Lizzie thought him a complete idiot. What did she expect him to say when she announced the client wanted to throw their deal out the window and renegotiate?

Sure, you can screw me over. I'll let you.

No way would he roll over and play dead. He wouldn't go down without one helluva fight. Not when his mom's life was at stake.

Rory carefully folded his napkin and placed it on the table.

A deal was a deal. "I specifically asked you what this job would pay, and you told me thirty thousand. If there was a chance the job would pay less, that was the time to tell me."

Elizabeth paled.

Good. No way would he make this comfortable or easy for her.

"In my own defense, I discussed the issue with Devlin, and thought we were clear on this." She shifted uncomfortably in her chair. "Yesterday was the first time he mentioned not wanting to pay you that amount."

"He needs to honor our agreement, and so do you."

Rory prided himself on conducting his business honestly and above reproach. Obviously, Devlin possessed fewer scruples.

"While you and I had discussed your monetary compensation, until a contract is signed there isn't a formal agreement in place with the client, and renegotiation is possible."

"Is this how he does business?"

"I've never had a problem like this with him before."

"I'm just lucky then."

"I don't blame you for being upset."

He couldn't let her know how important this job was to him, but he couldn't let her and Devlin screw him on the deal, either. "I'm past upset. I'm about ready to tell the guy to go to hell."

"Then we'll both be out of a job."

"And Devlin will be out of a spokesperson." Rory leaned back in his chair. "He'll have to start his search all over."

"Everybody loses then. What good does that do?"

"It'll make me feel damn good. I won't play the fool."

"No one is doing that. This is a business decision. You have to prove to Devlin that you'll increase sales enough to justify what he's paying you. If you had modeling experience, you could point to previous campaigns, and what they'd done for the company."

"Just because I don't have the numbers to prove it doesn't mean I won't bring in money."

"I agree. In fact, I'm banking on that very fact, but Micah Devlin is a numbers man. If he can't see it on paper, it doesn't exist."

"Is this a deal breaker for Devlin?"

"I honestly don't know, but it very well could be. He mentioned that cowboys had to be a dime a dozen."

"I don't see a whole lot of them in New York City." Rory waved his arm around the room. "You see a lot of cowboys here?"

"I tried all these arguments with Devlin. Between you and me, and if you mention this to anyone I'll deny it, I don't agree with what he's doing."

"But here you are, asking me to work for less."

"Devlin Designs is my client. I have to respect the CEO's wishes." Her finger drew lines in the condensation on her water glass. "If you want to keep your job, the best thing to do is agree to Devlin's demands."

"I've met this kind of businessman before. He doesn't care who he plows over as long as the deal works out well for him."

"Help me out here." Elizabeth leaned forward and placed her small hand on his forearm.

Her simple touch sent off shock waves through his system stronger than a kick from an unbroken horse, momentarily sending him into a giant fog.

"I sense we both want to find a solution to this problem," she continued. "I don't want to see you get screwed, but Devlin's met with other agencies. He could go with someone else."

"I can't take less money." If Rory gave in now, Devlin would try to screw him again somewhere down the road. "I do more than give tours. I breed horses. Sometimes on paper a foal doesn't look like he'll be anything out of the ordinary. Then when I work with him I see something special, something I can't put a finger on. You know those intangibles you were talking about."

She nodded.

"When I come across a horse like that, I'm going to drive a hard bargain when I sell him. What I'm saying is I'm an experienced horse trader. No one's going to take advantage of me."

AT NINE-FIFTY THE NEXT MORNING, Elizabeth met Rory in the agency reception area and ushered him to her office, closing the door behind them. A night of worry and anger threatened to choke her. "Please tell me you've changed your mind about your salary demands."

Rory shook his head. "The man told you he'd pay me thirty. That's what you told me. A deal's a deal."

She hated stubborn men. She ought to put Rory and Devlin in a room and let them fight it out, because she'd had enough of both of them.

"There's nothing I can do to talk you out of this?"

"Nope."

She reminded herself to breathe. Maybe when faced with Rory's defiance, Devlin would back down.

Sure, and as Chloe often said, pigs would fly.

At least Rory was dressed like the cowboy spokesman Devlin wanted. He wore the same navy shirt he'd worn when they'd met, plus his boots and his royal flush belt buckle. "I'm glad you had the common sense to wear the client's jeans."

"Don't give up, Lizzie." He reached out to her, but at the last minute pulled back and shoved his hand in his pocket. "You might be surprised how this meeting turns out."

His smooth, cool voice wrapped around her, and the confidence in his eyes almost had her believing him. Wait a minute. How could he remain this calm and collected unless he was up to something?

"Tell me you don't have some harebrained scheme planned."

"Would I do that?"

"I don't know you well enough to answer that question." Elizabeth shook her head. "No, that's not true. I suspect you'd try just about anything to get your way."

"Harebrained ideas aren't my style."

These two men were going to kill her. Either that or drive her completely insane if she didn't rein them in. But before she could respond, her office phone buzzed. She reached around Rory, grabbed her phone and answered the inside line.

After ending the call, she picked up her Netbook off her desk. "Devlin's waiting. Don't try anything we'll both regret. He's a very astute businessman and doesn't like to be questioned."

"I wouldn't dream of it."

"I recognize sarcasm when I hear it, and I don't appreciate it. At least listen to what the man has to say. He's always been reasonable in the past."

"I have to do what's right."

"Please…" She reached out and placed her hand on his forearm. Muscles rippled under her palm, sending corresponding waves ricocheting through her. "Remain open-minded."

A second later he broke the contact. As she and Rory walked toward the conference room, she couldn't help but think she was heading into a business meeting that would end in a pissing match. As the only non-testosterone-filled party present, she'd be utterly doomed.

When they entered the conference room, she introduced the two men and they shook hands.

"I don't believe in running around the mountain," Rory said as he sank into a leather chair across from Devlin at the conference table. "I climb straight to the top. I heard you had concerns about the campaign."

Elizabeth cringed as she sat beside Devlin and booted up her Netbook. Hadn't the cowboy ever heard of small talk and tact? She turned to Devlin. "Rory and I met last night." She tossed him an I-talked-with-him-like-you-told-me-to look. "I shared some of your concerns regarding the campaign."

"My first concern has been addressed," Devlin said. "I wanted to make sure your voice will work in commercials and in public appearances."

"I'm glad we have that settled." Elizabeth retrieved the file containing her notes. "Rory and I discussed him doing spots on morning shows." She glanced at her file to refresh her fuzzy, sleep-deprived brain, then swiveled her chair toward Devlin. "Rory's had experience with the local media. Morning shows won't be his first interview situation. Also, his work with tourists from all over the world has taught him to deal with unusual situations and to think on his feet."

She smiled. Could she spin a situation or what?

"National morning shows are very different from being interviewed by local reporters," Devlin said.

Rory leaned forward in his chair and braced his elbows on the table. "People are people. I figure if I treat these high-priced morning show hosts with respect, I ought to do fine."

Respect? Sirens blared in Elizabeth's head, sensing where Rory's thoughts had turned. Her mind scrambled to determine a way to derail him before he blasted Devlin. *Say anything. Just get the words out before Rory does.* "That attitude will definitely come across on TV, and people will relate to Rory for that. Don't you agree, Micah?"

"I have a lot riding on this campaign," Devlin said to Rory.

"As long as I represent your company, in public no one will see me in jeans other than yours."

"As it should be."

Rory nodded. "I'll talk up the product. I can tour the rodeo circuit. I know a few boys that might be able to get us some publicity in that market. What you see here is what you get. I pride myself on honesty."

Elizabeth opened her mouth to say something, but snapped it shut instead, deciding to sit back and watch the show. Rory had said he was an experienced horse trader. He hadn't been joking. The cowboy was holding his own with Devlin. No small accomplishment, considering Devlin held an MBA.

"I expect the same from you," Rory added. "Which brings me to the issue of money. We had a verbal agreement regarding my payment, and now you're going back on your word."

"This is business, and until there's a signed contract, everything is negotiable." Devlin straightened in his chair. "With your experience, thirty thousand for a campaign is a bit high."

"I'm worth every penny." Rory leaned forward.

The man's confidence astounded her, and was in fact a thing of beauty to watch.

"There's a fine line between confidence and arrogance." Devlin's hands tightened around the upholstered chair arms as he glared at him.

"I have a proposition for you," Rory said, clearly unfazed by Devlin's harsh look. "I did some checking on the internet last night. From what I gathered, a spokesman is usually paid every time pictures are taken or a commercial is shot. Then he gets paid again when ads run in magazines, newspapers or on TV. He also gets paid more for interviews."

Devlin nodded.

Elizabeth sat back, somewhat shocked. Sure, people could discover just about anything on the web, but that didn't mean they understood what they read. Rory actually sounded as if he knew what he was talking about.

"From what I read, the spokesman makes more money that way than with a flat fee, but I read about something called a buyout. I'll sign a contract today for thirty grand."

Thin lines formed around Devlin's mouth. "I have no guarantee you can pull off interviews or a TV commercial. I'm taking all the risk here."

"Then I'll have my agent call you."

Rory's little gem of news hit Elizabeth right between the

eyes. Anger clogged her throat. Agent? How dare he not mention he'd signed with someone?

Wait a minute. Rory couldn't have gotten an agent in the last two days. She relaxed. He was bluffing, and doing a damned good job of it.

Devlin's angry eyes pinned Elizabeth like a butterfly in a child's science project. "You said he was representing himself."

"That's what I was told."

"If money's going to be an issue, we can stop things right here. I'll get an agent, and you can deal with him." Rory crossed his arms over his broad chest. His determined gaze drilled into Devlin. "Who would you rather negotiate with? I'm guessing it's me, but the choice is up to you."

Elizabeth held her breath and waited. She'd just witnessed horse trading at its finest.

"I'm willing to go as high as twenty-five, but I want the payments made in thirds over the course of the contract."

"I want half up front forty-eight hours after I sign the contract."

"Deal, but I want everything we've agreed to today put into the contract." Devlin held out his hand, and he and Rory shook on it.

Miracles did happen. Elizabeth closed her eyes to hide her relief. When she opened them, she reached for her Netbook. "I'll write up the contract terms as negotiated, and let you both review it. Then you can send it to your legal department, Micah."

Both men nodded.

"I'll have the agency's contract to you later today," Devlin told Elizabeth. He turned to Rory. "If you give me your email address, I'll send you our contract with you. I'd like to have it signed by early next week so we can proceed with the campaign."

"I'll sign it as soon as I have a lawyer look over it."

Ten minutes later, a slightly shell-shocked Elizabeth escorted both men to the reception area. Once Devlin left, she faced Rory. "You should have told me what you intended to do."

"If I had, would you have trusted me?"

"No."

"That's why I didn't tell you."

"While your show was entertaining, and you came up with a good solution that benefited everyone, don't ever pull something like that again."

A WEEK LATER Rory thought he'd lost his mind. All he did was stand around and let people take pictures of him all day, and sit around the hotel watching any sports event he could find on TV all night.

He'd talked to Griff a few times. The first time, he'd called to get an update and make sure Devlin's check cleared. So far, his little brother was doing a fine job managing the ranch in his absence. Not being missed there had been a tough pill to get down.

Restless and needing to see the sky above his head, Rory decided to take a walk. He missed being outside, being active. He'd tried working out in the hotel gym, and that helped some, but he needed to feel fresh air and the sun on his skin. Remembering his agreement with Devlin, he pulled off his worn Wranglers and tossed on the designer jeans before grabbing his hat and heading out.

The list of reasons he'd be happy once this gig was over kept growing, starting with the jeans. He'd never liked the blasted things no matter how much he wore them, and they still made him feel like a sissy.

He hadn't walked a block when his cell phone rang.

"Thought I'd let you know we signed the papers for Jameson to buy Star's foal."

Good. That would help the ranch's cash flow. "Don't let him

pick up the foal until you've got confirmation the money's been transferred into our accounts."

"Got it."

"You're doing a good job, little brother."

Had he made it too easy for his siblings, always stepping in to take care of things when the situation got the slightest bit tough? Rory had thought he was helping. Being the oldest, he'd learn everything the hard way. He hadn't wanted his younger siblings to go the same route.

"I don't know how you do it. Managing this place is sure cramping my style. I was so damned tired last night I fell asleep at ten o'clock."

Rory laughed. "Not so easy to be the life of the party when you've got to get up at dawn."

"How are things going on your end?"

"It's been a long week." Rory rubbed his stiff neck.

"So modeling's not all bright lights and pretty girls?"

"It's hard work. I'm already tired of people telling me what to do."

Griff chuckled. "Getting a chance to see how the other half lives, huh?"

"Can't say I like it a whole lot." Rory stopped at the corner of Broadway and Forty-ninth and waited for the light to change. He'd learned early on that these New York City drivers would just as soon run someone over as stop to avoid him. "You heard from Mom? I called last night, but she was asleep. Avery says she's holding her own, but the treatment's tough on her."

"Avery said it's worse than chemo."

As long as the treatment didn't kill her, but killed the cancer. "Keep me posted."

He ended the call. People rushed past him. Everyone here lived in such a hurry. No wonder Elizabeth fit right in. The woman was a whirlwind. Would she act like that in everything she did—that is, if she ever loosened up? If she focused that energy on a man, she could burn him to cinders in the bed. Rory smiled. What a way to go.

Someone bumped into him, mumbled a quick apology and scooted off. This walk wasn't accomplishing what he'd hoped. Instead of releasing his pent-up energy, being out on the streets had spiked his blood pressure.

He missed the quiet at home. When he hiked in the mountains, he could think. The solitude cleared his head. Whenever he took a walk here, he returned to the hotel with a headache.

He'd hoped the streets might be quiet this early in the morning, but no such luck. Neon lights flashed. Horns honked constantly. People hurried by. He glanced upward, hoping a glimpse of the sky would calm his nerves. Instead, the Times Square billboard caught his gaze. He froze.

No. It couldn't be.

Lizzie never mentioned anything about a billboard. He stared. No matter how hard he tried, he couldn't deny the reality slapping him in the face.

Chapter Seven

There he was, big as the Rocky Mountains, wearing nothing but the blasted fancy designer jeans and his cowboy hat, his arms crossed over his chest for all the world to see. The words *Devlin jeans, strong enough for a real man* ran along the bottom of the billboard.

He scoffed. Leave it to Lizzie to come up with that slogan. As if any real man would wear these jeans....

And how in the heck did she get the blasted billboard done so fast?

He'd thought the photo shoot had been embarrassing. Seeing himself staring down from a billboard sent him skyrocketing to new heights of humiliation. How would he ever handle television commercials airing on stations in his neck of the woods? At least no one he knew would see this.

Think about the money and Mom. That would get him through.

"Is that you up there?"

He turned to find a twentysomething brunette, her hair pulled into a ponytail and a Texas Rangers baseball hat perched on her head, ping-ponging between him and the billboard.

"It is," her friend, dressed in jeans and an I love NY T-shirt, said. "He's wearing the same jeans, and look, he's got the same poker hand belt buckle."

"Yup, it's me." Unfortunately.

"Are you famous?"

"No." *Please, Lord, let this be the extent of my fame. Don't even give me fifteen minutes. That's way too much.*

"I bet you'll be famous soon," I Love NY said, her eyes glued on him as if he were the only stallion in the pasture.

Some men would think this scenario was a dream come true. "That's kind of you to say so," he mumbled.

I Love NY dug through her purse. A second later she handed him a Starbucks receipt and a pen. "Can I have your autograph?"

He almost asked her if she was kidding, before the manners his mother had drilled into his thick skull kicked in. "I'd be happy to. What's your name?"

"Lindsay."

He wrote "To Lindsay, thanks for being my first fan," and signed his name. This autograph stuff wasn't so bad. He might even grow to like it. "You ladies from New York?"

"We're here on a girls' vacation. We're from Texas."

"I should've guessed that." He pointed to the baseball cap.

The other woman handed him a scrap of paper. "My name's Judy."

He stood there trying to figure out something clever to write. Signing autographs was harder than a person would think unless he simply scrawled his name, or wrote something generic. He thought doing that was kind of a raw deal. Everybody liked to feel special. He finally settled on "Judy, enjoyed meeting you in NYC" and signed his name.

When he looked up from the scrap of paper, a crowd of women had gathered and started tossing questions at him.

"Are you married?"

"No." Someone else shoved paper and pen into his hand. "Who should I make—"

"Seeing anyone?"

An image of Lizzie flashed before his eyes. How insane was

that? The last thing he needed was a relationship with another city woman. "Not right now."

He scrawled his name on the paper and held it out. To heck with making them feel special. He just wanted to get out of here. This many women, all focused on him, couldn't be good. One woman was unpredictable—a gaggle of them downright scary.

"Do you have any pictures?"

"Not right—"

"Do you live in New York?"

These women could teach police interrogation classes.

"I live in Colorado."

"Here's my business card," a tall blonde dressed in black pants and a blouse said. "Call me. We can go out to dinner."

"Would you like me to show you around the city? Here's *my* business card."

Wonderful, he could start a collection. He managed to toss a smile in the general direction from which the card came.

The circle around him grew tighter. He backed up, bumped into a woman and mumbled a quick apology. A tall redhead leaned toward him. "You and I could have a lot of fun. Let's get out of here."

He considered telling her he was gay, just to get rid of her. But with the way his luck was going, she'd club him over the head and kidnap him to prove he wasn't, that he just hadn't met the right woman.

Before he could answer, the ladies all started talking at once, creating quite a noise. To the general crowd he blurted out, "Excuse me, I've got to go."

But when he stepped forward to leave, the circle didn't budge, and someone grabbed his arm. Fear shot through him. The women had him so surrounded that if he pulled away, he'd knock half of them down.

He turned to the heavyset woman at his elbow and smiled.

"Would you mind letting go of my arm? I'm thinking I might need it later today."

She leaned closer, and the bitter smell of coffee assailed him. "I'm from Littleton. Where in Colorado are you from?"

"I'm from Estes Park."

Another woman grabbed his left arm. His fear spiked up a notch. "Ladies, if you don't let go, you're going to pull me apart like a wishbone."

"Only if you agree not to go anywhere."

Right now he'd agree to just about anything to get these two to free him. "I can stick around awhile."

Apparently satisfied with his promise to stay, the women released him.

But when an escape route presented itself he'd be outta here faster than a jackrabbit with a coyote on its tail. Only who knew how long one would take to appear?

Then someone pinched him on the ass. He jumped and spun around, looking for the guilty party, not quite sure what to do if he identified her.

He drew the line at grabby women. His chest tightened and his heart banged painfully against his ribs. It was either him or them, because he couldn't take this anymore. Deciding to call in reinforcements rather than trample the women as he broke free, he grabbed his cell phone and called Lizzie. "I need your help."

"What's wrong?"

A woman shoved a Wal-Mart receipt and a pen into his hand. "Will you sign an autograph for me?"

"Do you have any pictures like the one on the billboard to sign?" someone else yelled. "I'd love one of those."

He tried to tune out the barrage of questions. "They've got me surrounded. You have to help me get back to the hotel."

"Who?"

"What hotel are you staying at?" someone shouted at him.

They could torture him for days, but no way would he give out that information.

"Women have me surrounded," he said, cupping his hand, still clutching the now sweaty pen and paper, around his ear in an attempt to hear better. "There's a whole herd of them. They're asking for my autograph. They're asking if I have pictures like the billboard. I don't know what to do, and they won't let me leave."

"This is fantastic!"

"No, it's not." A camera flash went off in his face, momentarily blinding him. Great. Now he was completely defenseless.

"We have a few photos of the billboard shot. I'll be there with them in ten minutes. This is exactly the kind of reaction we want."

"I'm glad one of us is happy, but you'd better get here sooner than ten minutes."

"Whatever you do, be nice. Keep people talking, and try to get them to stay. As often as you can, mention Devlin's men's jeans and that they're available at department stores."

He was in the middle of a feeding frenzy, and Lizzie was worried about how often he mentioned the product? Didn't her business mind ever take a day off?

He and Griff had often fought over the last cookie in the jar. More often than not, the treat had ended up in pieces. Rory never dreamed he'd one day know how the cookie felt.

CLUTCHING A HANDFUL of photos and wearing a huge smile, Elizabeth hurried to Times Square. Rory said a crowd had gathered. She should've asked him how many people were there. He lived in a town of seven thousand, so probably thought ten people constituted a crowd.

Her mind raced, trying to develop ways to capitalize on the situation. Hopefully, people would still be there when she arrived. That way they could keep the impromptu autographing going. If she got lucky, and it was a slow news day, maybe a local channel would stop by.

Why leave the situation to chance? Make it happen, but not with the local stations. The *Wake Up America* studio sat right on Times Square. She pulled out her phone and called a reporter on the show that she'd met at a breast cancer awareness event she'd attended last year. "Brooke, have you seen the new Times Square billboard?"

"Is it one of yours?"

"Sure is, and this cowboy's a dream."

"I'll have to check it out."

"My guy's there now, and from what I hear, he's gathering quite a crowd. Women are already recognizing him." Elizabeth sped up and dodged a cab. "If it's a slow day, it could make a cute filler piece on tomorrow's show. Colorado cowboy takes the big city by storm."

"Trolling for free publicity again?"

"This could be mutually beneficial. Rory's the new spokesman for Devlin's men's jeans. He's going to be hot. You could be the first show to interview him."

She turned the corner onto Broadway and spotted a crowd of at least thirty women. "Got to go. Trust me. Get over here. You don't want to miss out on this."

Adrenaline shot through Elizabeth's system. She couldn't have orchestrated a better scenario. Rushing forward, she started handing out Rory's photo to women, and shoved a Sharpie into his hand.

"Get me out of here," he pleaded, his eyes wide with fear.

She almost laughed. The man towered above the women and outweighed most of them by at least fifty pounds.

"No way. We're making the most of this."

He leaned down and his warm breath tickled her ear. "They're getting grabby. I've been pinched three times."

She couldn't hold back her laughter this time. To these women Rory probably looked like a piece of chocolate cake at a Weight Watchers meeting. "You'll survive. Sometimes you've got to take one for the team."

He glared at her. "The team damned well better appreciate this."

"Duly noted."

Part of her did feel sorry for him. Models expected this kind of thing and had experience dealing with public appearances. Rory was completely out of his element. She made a mental note to prep him for these types of public situations. Her instincts told her this wouldn't be the last time someone recognized him.

"Ladies, Rory will be glad to talk to all of you. If you could just move back a little bit to give him some breathing room, that would be great."

While he signed autographs and answered personal questions, she told everyone they could find Devlin's men's jeans at most department stores. She and Rory made a pretty good team. Once they returned to the office, she'd call Devlin to tell him Rory had been recognized from the billboard, and that the reaction he'd received had been exactly what they'd hoped for.

The situation went great for about ten minutes. Then suddenly, a fortysomething woman dressed in skintight jeans and a rhinestone T-shirt cupped her hand around Rory's magnificent butt and goosed him. He jumped, his panicked gaze locking with Elizabeth's.

She placed her palm gently on the diva's arm. "Please treat Rory with respect."

"Are you accusing me of something?"

The woman tugged her arm free at the same time Elizabeth removed her hand. Elizabeth flew backward, knocking into part of the crowd. Coffee rained down.

Another woman grabbed Rory. The brittle sound of tearing material filled Elizabeth's ears. Glancing at him, she saw his shirtfront was ripped from the pocket to the waist, revealing his bronzed, toned chest.

The noise grew deafening. Women yelled about getting splashed with coffee. Some screamed as they fell to the sidewalk. Others threatened to trample them. Women lunged at Rory.

Elizabeth reached for the fallen ones. "Watch out. Don't step on anyone," Rory said as he helped a middle-aged lady to her feet.

Women shoved each other, trying to get away or to get to Rory. An even bigger crowd grew as passersby stopped to watch the scene. It looked like one of those old films, with the blundering cops falling over each other.

What had she done?

"This wasn't what I had in mind," Elizabeth said as she helped another woman to her feet.

"You didn't mean to start a catfight?" Rory asked.

She shook her head. "What do we do? How do I stop this?" She had experience creating buzz, not shutting it down.

"Running comes to mind."

A whistle blew, immediately halting the chaos.

"Who started all this?" a policeman asked as he approached.

Every person except Rory pointed to Elizabeth.

"Officer, this is all a terrible misunderstanding," she said, desperate to diffuse the situation and pacify the cop. "A crowd had gathered. People got a little close. Someone bumped into someone else, and then everything went crazy."

"Everything was fine until she got here," the woman in the rhinestone T-shirt yelled.

What was it with her? Did she wake up this morning intent on destroying someone's life, and Elizabeth held the lucky ticket?

"Everyone seems pretty clear you're the instigator. Start at the beginning with why a crowd had gathered," the officer told Elizabeth.

She paused, not quite sure what to say. Police frowned on impromptu advertising events. They were sticklers for permits and advance notice. Both of which she'd forgotten in her excitement.

"Women started asking me for autographs when they recognized me from this," Rory said, pointing upward.

The officer glanced at the billboard. "Nice photo." He turned to Elizabeth. "Were you one of the autograph seekers?"

"I work with Rory."

"In what capacity? Are you his agent?" The man glared at her disapprovingly.

What she wouldn't give to be beamed out of this situation. Or to have the ability to erase everyone's memory, starting with this cop and the question he'd just asked. Because unless she lied, her answer would not make him happy.

She swallowed hard and prayed she could talk her way out of this sticky situation. "I'm not his agent. I'm the executive in charge of the ad campaign."

"You decided to stage an impromptu advertising event," the officer accused. "You thought you could get some free publicity without the hassle of getting the proper permits. When are you ad people going to realize you can't do that?"

"I absolutely did not stage this."

"I was feeling a little cooped up this morning, so I took a walk," Rory said. "When the crowd gathered I called Elizabeth to help me."

"What happened when you arrived?"

"She passed out pictures for him to sign, and started bossing everyone around," one woman, probably the diva, said.

"She bumped into me and spilled coffee all over me," another added.

The officer raised his hands, silencing everyone. "I've heard enough. I'm giving you and cowboy guy tickets for disturbing the peace, unlawful assemblage, failure to obtain the proper permits, and anything else I can think of. This little stunt is going to cost your company a bundle, little lady."

"That's all you're going to do?" someone called out.

"You should arrest her for assault," another woman added.

"That might not be a bad idea."

If this kept up these women would get her life in prison. Talk about a mob mentality.

Rory glanced at the officer. "Can I speak to you alone, man to man?"

The cop nodded and motioned to the crowd. "The rest of you, break it up. If your clothes were damaged, get a business card from her."

When he pointed at Elizabeth, she said, "I'll be happy to pay for dry cleaning or replace any garments that can't be cleaned."

As she handed out business cards and the crowd dispersed, Rory said, "This is my fault. I'm new to all this stuff. A few weeks ago I was in Colorado giving horseback riding tours. Now here, today, I was surrounded by a group of women wanting my autograph. It's a little much for a simple cowboy to handle. They got very close, if you know what I mean."

The officer laughed. "I can see that from your shirt."

"That wasn't the only place they got grabby." Rory shuddered. "They damn near scared me to death. I tried to leave, but they circled around me. The only way I could've escaped was to run the ladies over, but I was raised to treat women right."

Elizabeth watched in amazement as the officer's posture relaxed the longer he spoke with Rory. Give them five more minutes and they'd probably be fast friends.

The cop tilted his head toward Elizabeth. "What about her?"

"I called her. The crowd kept asking me for pictures, and I figured that if she brought some, they'd take the photos and go."

"You promise me nothing like this will ever happen again?"

"It won't, because if it did, it'd probably kill me."

The officer nodded and then turned to Elizabeth. "I want

one of your business cards, because if I hear you've been involved in something like this again, I won't just ticket you. I'll
haul you off to jail."

As Lizzie and Rory walked into her office, his anger threatened to boil over. If he was back home, he'd saddle Blaze and
head for the mountains, hoping a long ride would clear his
head and cool his temper. If that didn't work, he'd muck out a
few stalls to burn off steam. Unfortunately, none of those options were available.

As Lizzie sank into her leather desk chair, he realized his
best alternative would be putting his fist through her office
wall.

She, on the other hand, had been a little ball of excited
energy once she'd found out they weren't going to jail or getting ticketed.

"Tell me this kind of thing doesn't happen a lot," he finally
said, once he'd calmed down enough to speak.

"Why are you so upset? Everything turned out fine, but you
look like you're ready to hit something."

"Don't tempt me." Rory rested his fists on her desk. "You're
wondering why I'm upset? We nearly got arrested. I don't
know about you, but that's never happened to me before."

"But thanks to you, we weren't."

Only because he'd aw-shucked his way out of trouble. Not
one of his proudest moments. He'd handled the situation only
because he was doing this for his mom. If he wanted to live
in a big city and be in crowds all the time, he'd have gone to
Boston with Melissa.

Elizabeth swiveled toward her computer and punched a few
keys.

"Did you see all the people videoing the scene on their
phones? This is wonderful." She typed something on her key-
board. "I'm checking to see if it's on YouTube yet."

Rory shook his head. Had he heard her right? She couldn't have described the horror they'd just experienced as wonderful. "You're saying that there's no such thing as bad publicity?"

"Exactly." She spun her chair back around to face him. "It's not on YouTube yet, but I bet it will be tonight."

The sparkle in her ocean-blue eyes captivated him and took his anger down a notch or two. "Promise me this will never happen again."

"Gee, now I'll have to cancel the near riot I had scheduled for tomorrow."

He glared at her, more out of principle than genuine anger. "Very funny. It's easy for you to joke about this. You didn't almost get your clothes ripped off."

"I'm sorry. I should've anticipated someone recognizing you from the billboard. If I had prepared you more, the situation wouldn't have gotten so out of hand."

"Next time I head out I'm either taking a guard dog or going on horseback for a quick getaway."

When she laughed, the warm rich sound filled him, evaporating the last of his irritation. "I'm sorry there's no room in the campaign budget for those items."

"If I'd known the risks, I'd have added them to my contract demands."

His gaze locked with hers. Something passed between them. Something Rory hadn't expected and didn't want to examine. Lizzie was wrong for him in so many ways, and the timing couldn't be worse.

Her cell phone rang, thankfully breaking the spell. He'd been just about to make a very wrong turn.

Elizabeth could barely contain her excitement when caller ID revealed her contact from *Wake Up America* on the line. While she wouldn't have planned a scenario like the one in Times Square, she certainly planned to make the most of the free publicity.

"I heard your new model is so hot he caused a riot," Brooke said.

"I told you he was going to be big. What can I say? Women go wild for this guy."

"We'd love to interview your cowboy. Have him at the studio by 5:00 a.m."

Between prepping him and proofing the material for the print ads that had to go out first thing in the morning, Elizabeth would be up all night. The things she gave up for the job. But who needed sleep, anyway? Getting more than four hours a night was highly overrated.

"He'll be there." She ended the call. "*Wake Up America* wants to interview you. Their studios are at Times Square. It seems everyone's talking about you."

"Will they expect me to talk about what happened? If they do, I'm not too clear on things. All I remember is all these women surrounding me, and let me tell you, there's nothing scarier than a herd of angry, grabby women. My whole life flashed before my eyes."

"My first tip is not to refer to the women as an angry herd, or you might find yourself facing another one." For the first time since she'd met Rory, uncertainty briefly flashed in his eyes. How surprising that a group of women put a kink in his armor. "Just remember to utilize that cowboy charm I've seen you wield so often."

"Cowboy charm?" He flashed her a grin that could sell whiskey to a teetotaler.

"Give Brooke that look that mesmerizes a woman, and makes her think you're going to grab her, toss her on your horse and ride off into the sunset."

"Do I do that for you?"

His warm, husky voice rippled through Elizabeth as he leaned forward in his chair and peered into her eyes. He had the slightest smile on his face. Oh, yeah, that was the look.

Horse and sunset, here I come.

"Apparently I have cowboy immunity. Must've been included in my childhood shots, because I don't get why women go all wild for you cowboys."

"If you took a chance, you might be surprised."

Her mouth went dry. Her mind went blank. Her heart raced. This man was dangerous. He could get her to forget everything, including her own name.

Sometimes in the middle of the night when she couldn't sleep, she imagined letting go, of not living her life so tied to rules. She dreamed of finding a man—lately more often than not, Rory—to love her, but then reality crashed down.

"It takes a lot to surprise me."

"Is that a challenge?"

Sirens blared in her head. This game had gotten way out of control. The last thing she wanted was him thinking she'd challenged his manhood. Talk about waving a red cape in front of a bull. "We have a professional relationship, nothing more."

Maybe if she told herself that enough, she'd believe it.

He grinned. "If you say so, Lizzie."

"It's Elizabeth," she snapped, angry more over his comment than the use of his nickname for her. But the way he said it, combined with the way he looked at her, as if she were the scoop of ice cream on a slice of apple pie, made her toes curl. "Why do you persist in calling me Lizzie when I've asked you repeatedly not to?"

"It lights a fire in you, and puts the prettiest pink color in your cheeks."

Lit a fire in her? More toe curling. How could she be mad at him when he said that? "Of course it puts color in my cheeks. Calling me Lizzie makes me angry, or haven't you noticed?"

"I've noticed. It just doesn't bother me."

This man refused to be put in his place, scaring the hell out of her.

She stiffened, and reached for a file on her desk to keep her hands from shaking.

He stood and moved closer to her desk. His large body filled her vision. His musky scent wrapped around her. She inhaled deeply, then stopped herself, remembering that Rory didn't fit any of the criteria on her ideal-man checklist. In fact, he'd top her don't-date-this-kind-of-man list. So why did she find herself thinking about him way more than she should, and not in a businesslike manner, but in a very intimate way?

"You know what John Lennon said?" he asked.

"No, but obviously you're dying to enlighten me."

"Life is what happens while you're busy making other plans." Rory braced his hands on her desk and leaned close enough for her to notice he had the longest eyelashes she'd ever seen. "You're so busy making plans that you're missing out on life, Lizzie."

"I am not," she insisted lamely.

Terrific comeback, Elizabeth. That'll put him in his place.

"Saying it doesn't make it so."

"We need to prep for your interview tomorrow on *Wake Up America*," she said, pointedly ignoring his comment and desperately needing to reclaim control of the discussion. "What I think is—"

He straightened. "I need a hot shower after all those women pawed me."

"This can't wait—"

"Sure it can. Meet me at my hotel room at six. We can order room service and deal with the interview stuff over dinner."

"Meet me in front of your hotel at six. I'll drop by in a taxi. We can pick up dinner and then head to my house to work."

No way would she be alone with him in a hotel room, where the only furniture would be a couple of tiny desk chairs and a king-size bed. Talk about risky business.

As ELIZABETH AND RORY SAT in the cab on their way to her neighborhood deli, she questioned the wisdom of taking him to her town house. That was her personal space, her haven, and while she worked at home a lot, this felt like crossing the streams in *Ghostbusters*—something unknown and probably not good.

"How about we pick up takeout and head back to the office to work?"

"I've had enough of that place. If I'm working tonight, I want to kick back and relax."

"My office is—"

"It's your place, my hotel or nothing." He crossed his arms over his chest and flashed her the stubborn look she'd come to detest.

"My place it is."

She could handle the situation. They'd eat and discuss tomorrow's interview. She'd talk to him about what to expect and how he should respond. Same business meeting, just different location.

By the time the cab let them off in her neighborhood, she felt more relaxed, more under control.

"Guess I can say I now know how sardines feel," Rory said when they walked inside the deli and the cluster of people closed around them.

"The crowd's actually a little light tonight."

"I'd hate to see the place on a busy night. How do people keep from getting trampled?"

"There's an elaborate set of rules guiding traffic flow. I had to take a course when I moved to the city."

Rory froze and stared at her wide-eyed.

"What?"

"Was that a joke?"

She nodded. "Why is that so surprising?"

That right eyebrow rose. "I'd begun to think you had your funny bone surgically removed."

A woman bumped into Rory and mumbled a hasty apology. He cringed. "I'm having flashbacks." Then he sniffed the air and held out his arm to Elizabeth. "Do I smell like women's perfume?"

She stepped closer, careful not to get too close, and inhaled. Nothing but clean, musky, intoxicating maleness filled her senses. Now that was a fragrance to drive women crazy.

"You definitely don't smell like perfume. Why?"

"Some of those grabby women must've bathed in the stuff. Even though I've taken a shower, I can still smell their perfume on me."

Visions of Rory in the shower, his hard body wet and glistening, flashed in Elizabeth's mind. Fantasies bombarded her. So much for being in control.

The man behind the counter asked what they wanted. What a loaded question, with Rory standing beside her and desire thrumming through her system. She couldn't think.

She'd thought being alone with him in his hotel room was risky business. As they walked out of the deli, Elizabeth realized she had no idea what she'd ordered for dinner. Apparently just being with Rory was dangerous, and she was taking him home.

Chapter Eight

Elizabeth had never thought of her town house as small until Rory walked in. He more than physically filled the space; his essence overwhelmed it. And he looked so comfortable, so at ease.

So much for her town house feeling less risky than his hotel room.

Trying desperately to harness her raging hormones, she headed for the safety of her kitchen. "You'll have to excuse the mess," she said as they entered. "I'm in the process of re-modeling."

She deposited the deli sack containing their dinners on the black granite counter, and shook her head in disgust. Only half the glass-and-stone backsplash had been installed. Except for the top one, the boxes of slate flooring hadn't been opened, and that was to have been installed today, as well. The project was already a week behind schedule. What had the tile guy done all day? Watch ESPN? "I can't believe it. They told me the backsplash and the floor would be done by now."

"You hired someone? They charge a fortune. Tiling isn't tough. You could've done the installation yourself."

No way would she do that kind of physical labor. "I went to college so I could make a good salary and pay people to do things like this for me." She stopped, embarrassed over what she'd said. Could she sound any more condescending to someone who worked with his hands? How much did ranch hands make, anyway? Probably not much. Maybe he only earned enough to scrape by. "That didn't come out right. I'm no good with power tools, and there's the whole learning curve thing, and time's an issue for me. I hired someone so the project would be done in a timely manner."

"If you did the work yourself you'd save a ton of money."

"You're obsessed with money," she countered. "I see it as my way of helping the economy by creating jobs."

Maybe Rory had grown up poor. People with his kind of money obsession often had. Even when they crawled out of poverty, they worried that one misstep would send them tumbling back.

"Your contractors left the tile adhesive." Rory pointed to a tub in the corner of the kitchen. "I could finish the backsplash in no time."

"I'm paying someone to do this."

"Fire him. He said he'd have the work done today, and he didn't. Did he call to say why he didn't finish?"

"I'm capable of managing this job."

"I'll take that as a no."

"Okay, so I need to stay a little more on top of things. I'll call the tile man tomorrow and find out what happened."

She pulled a bottle of cabernet out of the metal wine rack on the corner of her counter. "Want a glass of wine?" She definitely needed one. The man was driving her crazy, and she hadn't even started prepping him for the interview.

Rory nodded.

After opening the wine, she filled two crystal wineglasses and handed one to him. She took a big swallow before setting her glass on the counter. Scanning the directions on the lid of their entrées, she discovered they were having chicken Parmesan and bowtie pasta. "I don't cook much."

"Technically, you're not cooking now. You're reheating."

"I'm using the oven. As far as I'm concerned, that constitutes cooking." Elizabeth turned the dial to Bake and set the temperature for three hundred fifty degrees. "Do you want dinner or not? Keep in mind, those who criticize don't eat."

"Cooking it is."

A strange metallic odor filled the kitchen. "What's that awful smell?"

Rory smiled. What did he know that she didn't?

"Have you used the oven before?"

"No, it's new." Or was, three months ago.

"The oven gives off that smell the first time it's turned on."

She glared, annoyed at him for pointing out her ignorance. "How do you know that's what it is? Maybe I've got a gas leak or something."

"We bought my mom a new oven a couple years back. It gave off the same awful smell the first time she turned it on."

He had Elizabeth there. Her only culinary experience had occurred before the age of thirteen, with her grandmother, and those appliances had been ancient.

"Is it okay to use?"

"It's fine, but it'll stink for a while. Did you take the instruction manual out?"

"Damn." She grabbed the oven door and pulled, but it wouldn't budge. She tugged harder. Nothing. Now what?

Rory materialized beside her and peeled off the clear tape that held the oven door closed. Then he pulled out a plastic bag of paperwork. After tossing the packet into the sink, he stepped back.

Feeling like a complete fool, and thinking she should try out for the Food Network show *Worst Cooks in America,* she tossed the aluminum containers holding their dinners into the oven and slammed the door. "I've never gotten new appliances before."

"It sounds like you've done a lot to the place. How much of an equity boost will you get?"

"What do you know about that?"

"I know you have to make sure you don't put more money into a house than you'll get out when you sell it."

"I'll check with my designer on that."

"Check with a Realtor. The designer makes money off your remodeling. The more renovations, the more money she makes."

As Elizabeth moved around the kitchen, setting the table, the fact that he'd considered things she hadn't stung her pride. She was smart, and yet hadn't considered how much she was raising the value of her town house versus the renovation costs. She hadn't shopped around to get the best price on materials, either. How had she strayed so far from her usual thoroughness?

She'd forgotten those things because she'd been so desperate to make a home, a place that reflected her personality. A sanctuary that soothed her soul after a long day, and was truly hers. Something she'd missed since her grandmother died.

"You're so organized and in control in your job," Rory said. "You need to be the same with this project."

She smiled. "Was that a compliment?"

"Guess so."

Despite downplaying his praise, she found his words set off a warm glow inside her. He admired her as a businesswoman, but what did he think of her as a woman? *Don't go there.* Doing so would be like the dumb blonde in every horror movie that heard a funny noise, went to investigate and got killed by the psychopath. "Thank you. That means a lot to me, especially after today."

The oven timer beeped. She opened three drawers before locating the oven mitt Chloe had given her three years ago as a housewarming gift. Carefully, Elizabeth removed their dinners, plated them and placed them on her kitchen table.

"I thought we'd go over strategies for your interview while we eat."

"Woman, don't you ever take time off?"

"Tomorrow is important." She forced her voice to remain level and not to go into lecture mode, despite her annoyance. "It's your first national TV appearance. You need to be prepared."

"There's more to life than work. When do you loosen up and have fun?"

"I enjoy what I do."

"It's not the same thing. What about going out with friends? Spending time with family?"

His simple question unleashed that nagging little voice that had plagued her way too often lately. A picture of Nancy's tear-streaked face flashed in Elizabeth's mind. No, she wouldn't end up alone like that. She had time to find a good man, and weren't a lot of women doing just fine waiting until their late thirties before having children? So if that was true, why had his words caused her chest to tighten up?

"I have friends I socialize with," she insisted, though the words sounded hollow even to her.

She raised her chin in defiance, refusing to allow him to make her doubt her life. Two could play twenty questions. Time for Rory to be on the defensive. "You say all I care about is work, but all you seem to care about is money. What about that?"

"That is none of your business."

"Hurts to look in the mirror, doesn't it?"

"Since neither of us is perfect, how about we call it a draw?"

"Deal." She smiled. How could he so effortlessly pushed her buttons, and then equally as effortlessly deflate her irritation? Shaking herself mentally and remembering her goal for tonight, she said, "I know the situation today was hard for you personally, but don't you realize how amazing it was?"

Rory visibly shuddered. "I think what happened is going to give me nightmares."

"The reaction today means we can create an association in

people's minds between the product and you. When people see your face they'll think of Devlin jeans."

"Kind of like when people see Morris the Cat they think of Nine Lives cat food."

She laughed. "That's an interesting comparison. Wonder what that says about you?"

"I didn't say *I* was like Morris the Cat."

No way would she compare him to anything as tame as a house cat. A panther maybe, because all stretched out he appeared disinterested in the world, but in reality was keenly alert and ready to strike.

When they'd finished dinner and cleared the table, Elizabeth said, "To prepare, I thought I'd ask you possible interview questions. Then we'd go over ways you could answer."

"What a great way to spend an evening."

After refilling their wineglasses, they moved into the living room. As she sank onto her upholstered white couch and waited for Rory to get settled, she glanced around the room. The white sofa paired with the black chairs and a touch of red accents suited her minimalistic style perfectly. Then her gaze focused on Rory, and she found herself biting her lip to keep from laughing.

His muscular frame looked so ridiculously powerful as he squeezed into a small armchair. "Join me over here. That way we'll be closer, like you'll be with Brooke when she interviews you tomorrow."

Even though he sat on the other end of the couch, Rory's presence overwhelmed Elizabeth. His earthy scent swirled around her. What would her life be like with him there all the time?

What was she thinking? They worked together. Taking a deep breath and focusing on tonight's purpose, preparing him for tomorrow's interview, she said, "Today's journalism leans toward sensationalism. Don't be surprised if a lot of the questions are filled with sexual innuendos."

"What happened to serious journalism?"

"That's reserved for political leaders and crime victims."

"What kind of things will she ask?"

"She'll probably ask you things like what it felt like to have all those women wanting your attention."

"It felt damned scary."

"You can't say that. Say it was like nothing you'd ever experienced before."

He laughed. "That's for sure."

"She also might ask you about your pecs. What size they are, for example."

Rory's eyebrow rose at her comment. "Why would she do that?"

Elizabeth licked her lips. She couldn't say because his pecs were more intoxicating than Chloe's killer margaritas. "She'll probably ask about them because it's apparent from the billboard that you're in very good shape."

"This interview sounds like it'll be as much fun as dealing with those women in Times Square."

THE NEXT MORNING Elizabeth stood beside Rory in the *Wake Up America* studio for his first television interview. While bats had set up residence in her stomach and were playing a rousing game of tag, Rory appeared completely relaxed. Nothing seemed to bother the man. Elizabeth smiled to herself. *Except the crowd of women in Times Square.*

They'd met at four this morning for breakfast. While Rory shoveled down scrambled eggs, pancakes and bacon, she'd tossed out questions for him to answer. He'd done well, but would he do as well when the cameras were rolling? He wouldn't be the first person to freeze up in front of a TV camera.

Think positive. Send out good energy, Elizabeth. If you believe in him, he'll believe in himself.

"You'll do a great job in this interview. Be yourself, cowboy. When you do that you effortlessly captivate women."

He looked down at her. His brown eyes sparkled. "Do I captivate you, Lizzie?"

Her breath caught in her chest. When he focused on her as he was now, she felt she was the only woman in the world. If only it were true, and not that he looked at every woman that way. Where did reality begin and end with this man?

Then she realized he'd called her Lizzie.

She decided to ignore the name issue, since correcting him had become an exercise in futility. Maybe ignoring it would take the fun out of the game. "Remember, I said I'm immune to your cowboy charm."

Though she might need a booster shot soon. Very soon.

A production assistant informed Rory his interview was up after the next set of commercials. "Remember to be positive," Elizabeth whispered before the assistant ushered him onto the set.

Her iPhone rang. Pulling it out of her purse, Elizabeth checked the screen and noticed Nancy's name.

"I was going to call you later to tell you I've been saying extra prayers today." Her friend had another chemo treatment this morning.

"I need all the prayers I can get today," Nancy's weak voice whispered over the phone lines.

"Are you okay?" Elizabeth's heart tightened.

"That's why I'm calling. This is a bit of a rough day. Could you make sure Mark gets his art for the Hamlin furniture ad to the printer by five?"

"No problem. I'll see to it. You rest as much as you can."

"I keep repeating what you told me, that this is just a speed bump, but some days it's harder to believe than others."

"How about I bring you some dinner later?"

"I'd love some chicken soup from Cohen's."

"You got it." Elizabeth glanced at the set and noticed Brooke had joined Rory. "I've got to go. Rory's interview is about to start."

With his dark good looks and her tall golden appeal, the pair made a striking couple. An odd feeling twisted inside Elizabeth.

Once seated on the sofa, Rory started to remove his Stetson.

"Leave your hat on." Brooke placed her graceful hand on Rory's arm. "It makes you so much more cowboy."

Elizabeth rolled her eyes at how Brooke drew out the word *cowboy.* "I have to say, Rory, you're as attractive in person as you are on the Times Square billboard."

Then the reporter actually blushed.

Oh, please. How obvious could she be? She might as well ask Rory if he'd like to have a roll in the hay.

"That's kind of you to say, Brooke." Rory flashed the reporter his million-dollar smile.

Elizabeth shook her head. The man was a walking pheromone, mesmerizing any woman within twenty feet of him. He should wear a warning label. *Caution—may cause women to lose their faculties after prolonged exposure.*

The red camera lights came on. "If you've been in Times Square lately you've probably seen our next guest staring down at you from a billboard. He's the bare-chested cowboy wearing Devlin Designs' men's jeans," Brooke said. She turned to Rory. "You caused quite a stir yesterday."

"I was walking around right outside your studio and a couple of women recognized me from the Devlin Designs jeans billboard in Times Square. They asked me for my autograph, and then next thing I knew I was surrounded by women."

Elizabeth smiled, pleased that Rory remembered her instruction to mention the company name as often as possible.

"I hear a couple of the women got a little touchy-feely, if you know what I mean. Not that I blame them."

"I got to say, I'm not used to all this female attention. I'm just a simple cowboy from Colorado."

Elizabeth almost laughed again. Simple cowboy? After last night's discussion on home equity and remodeling, she suspected Rory was anything but. That man, however, had disappeared once they arrived at the studio. The Rory on the set was all aw-shucks. A regular good old boy. Which man was the real one?

"I noticed you didn't answer my question." Brooke's voice broke through Elizabeth's thoughts.

Red spread across Rory's cheeks. Elizabeth covered her mouth to hold back her laughter, unable to believe he actually blushed.

"I did receive a pinch or two, and my shirt got torn some."

"Did you know video of what happened yesterday has been posted on YouTube?"

After glancing at the floor for a few seconds, Rory returned his attention to Brooke and smiled. "Now that is something. I never thought I'd end up on YouTube."

Lizzie cringed. His posture had stiffened slightly and the smile didn't reach his eyes. He was truly embarrassed being on display. Part of her wished she could run onto the set and rescue him. Now that she'd seen him genuinely happy, as he'd been when he'd joked about her cooking skills, or lack thereof last night, watching him now bordered on painful.

"I've seen the clip," Brooke continued. "I think you're being modest about the reaction you received. Let's see what our viewers think."

A second later the sight of Rory surrounded by women popped up on the monitor. Elizabeth glanced at Rory, who stared at everything in the studio but the monitor as the scene played out. Seeing the video gave Elizabeth an entirely different perspective on the incident. While they'd been in the thick of things, she'd concentrated on making the most of the opportunity. For the first time she actually put herself in Rory's shoes, a man new to the city and the ad game.

The women touched his arm. A few placed their hands on his chest when they asked for his autograph. More than a couple had pinched his butt. One woman goosed him. Of course, Elizabeth had known all that had happened, but seeing it in a more detached way and all together, she realized how degrading the women's actions had been toward Rory.

And yet, through it all, he'd remained polite. A complete gentleman.

The YouTube clip ended, and Brooke turned to Rory, an impish grin on her face. "The women almost ripped your shirt completely off. Good thing you work for a clothing company. You might go through a lot of shirts."

Rory chuckled, the slightly harsh sound grating on Elizabeth's ears. "Who would've thought I should've asked for a replacement shirt clause in my contract with Devlin Designs?"

"How about you take off your shirt and show us your wonderful abs so our viewers can see what all the excitement was about?"

Rory froze. Brooke looked him up and down like a woman about to pounce.

Then his gaze sought out Elizabeth.

She shook her head and mouthed the words *you don't have to do this.* The last thing she wanted him to do was humiliate himself on national TV.

The humor that usually sparkled in his eyes had vanished, replaced with iron resolve as he stood and peeled off his shirt. Then he hooked his thumbs in his front pockets, leaned back on his heels, raised his chin a bit and stared straight at the camera. Nothing but confidence shone in his eyes. "Is this what you wanted to see?"

"Women across the country are certainly getting all hot and bothered right about now."

Rory flashed the reporter a forced smile and said, "I don't know about that."

"I do." Brooke cleared her throat. "That's all the time we have. Thanks for stopping by, Rory."

After she plugged the upcoming story and they went to commercial, Brooke said, "Interviewing you was a pleasure. If you want to get together and see some of the city's sights, call me." She pulled a business card out of her suit coat pocket and handed it to Rory once he'd shrugged on his shirt. "I'd be happy to play tour guide."

For Elizabeth the interview had been a triumph, but the success was bittersweet, because despite the charm and bravado he'd displayed, Elizabeth suspected the interview had cost Rory a large chunk of his pride.

AS HE WALKED OUT OF the *Wake Up America* studio, Rory didn't know how he could keep working for Devlin Designs and retain any semblance of who he was.

He'd do it because he loved his mother, of course, and she needed the money.

But he'd been wrong about the interview being as bad as the incident in Times Square. Yesterday's humiliation had been limited to under a hundred people. The interview had been far worse because he'd been treated like a sex object on national TV. People at home would see that show, and he'd never hear the end of it. He'd be the butt of jokes for years to come. Hell, he'd probably be in the old folks' home one day, and people would still be razzing him about appearing half-naked on *Wake Up America*.

"That was an experience," he said once they reached the street. Then he glanced at Lizzie. Her face glowed. The on-camera embarrassment had been worth it, to see the joy on her face now, and to know he'd put that look there.

"You were amazing." Lizzie threw her arms around him and hugged the stuffing out of him. Her unexpected praise combined with her luscious curves molded against his body had him alive and humming.

Her eyes shone with pride. In him. He felt himself drowning in her beautiful blue eyes. He'd slain her dragon for her. Power surged through him.

Desire scored a direct hit to his groin.

He lowered his lips to hers. One taste. What could that hurt? Yeah, and the captain of the *Titanic* probably said, "Don't worry. That's a small iceberg." Right before they hit the thing and sank.

Chapter Nine

Rory's lips covered hers, sending shock waves through her entire body. But that wasn't what excited Elizabeth the most. The shy man who'd bluffed his way through the interview and yet remained the perfect spokesman, polite and enthusiastic—had revealed an intoxicating strength of character far sexier than his great body.

His strong arms wrapped around her. She clutched his shirt, fearing her knees would give out.

Rory filled her senses. Her toes curled inside her Coach python printed pumps.

But immediately following those fantastic feelings, alarms blasted in her head. She tossed them and her never-mix-business-and-pleasure rule aside until her cell phone belted out Darth Vader's theme, and reality crashed down on her.

She jumped out of Rory's arms, her heart hammering as if she'd run three blocks, her body throbbing with desire. How had she gotten so completely lost in him? How could she have forgotten they were standing on the sidewalk in the middle of Times Square? This was so not good.

"Devlin's calling. Cross your fingers that he's as happy with the interview as we were." She avoided Rory's gaze as she said, "Hello, Micah. Did you see it?"

She tried to focus on his response, but her mind kept wandering back to Rory's kiss. How would she face him, work with him, now that they'd crossed that work-personal life boundary?

Right after her call with Devlin she needed to explain to Rory how she'd gotten carried away over his interview's success. She'd say they needed to keep things in perspective and remain professional.

"Our cowboy did a great job. He struck the right balance of country boy and confidence."

Elizabeth hailed a passing cab, and when Rory opened the door for her, she dived in. He sat in silence beside her, while she gave the driver her office address. "We set Rory up with a Twitter account a few days ago. I'll have him post a couple of tweets today." The cab driver blasted his horn at a couple pedestrians sauntering through the crosswalk.

"I hope this female fervor translates into jeans sales."

"I think it will. Women will be talking about the gorgeous guy they saw on *Wake Up America,* and they'll be heading to the nearest department stores to buy their guy a pair of Devlin's men's jeans."

"If the number of hits the video and our website have gotten since the interview are any indication, this campaign should be do well." Devlin paused. "I've been thinking."

Elizabeth cringed. Good things never happened for her when Micah Devlin said he'd been thinking. His ruminations invariably led to more work that needed to be accomplished immediately, or disastrous ideas she had to talk him out of. "What about?"

"Since meeting Rory, I've wondered about shooting the commercial in upstate New York. The setting doesn't seem to fit him. I checked out Estes Park on the internet. It's the perfect place to shoot the commercial."

She should have thought of that. Colorado and the Rocky Mountains were so a part of who Rory was. It added to his ruggedness, his appeal.

"Shooting the commercial in Colorado would increase the

production cost. When I'm back at the office, I'll run the numbers to see exactly what the change in location would add to the budget. We could go over everything tomorrow."

"No need. I want the commercial shot in Colorado on the ranch where Rory works. It'll add authenticity to the campaign. As soon as you get the details ironed out, I want to head to Colorado. I don't want to let the excitement wane. I want to get this commercial on the air as quickly as possible."

Sure, the major work for the commercial was done, but didn't he realize the script would need changes, and negotiating with the ranch owner would take time? She briefly considered mentioning those facts, but knew from past experience he'd only tell her to do whatever was necessary, within reason, of course, to get the job done. The man must think he owned her, body and soul. Either that or he thought she had nothing to do but work twenty-four hours a day on his campaign. "I'll get to work on hammering out the details once I get back to the office."

She gazed out the cab window, watching people bustle along the busy city sidewalks as the taxi sat stuck in traffic. The irony of the situation slapped her in the face. The pedestrians were moving faster than she was. Not only was she stuck in the cab, her entire life seemed stalled right now.

She worked her tail off for Rayzor Sharp Media, and in turn, for Devlin Designs, and all it seemed to get her was higher expectations, a pat on the head and no social life.

After Devlin instructed Elizabeth to email the shoot details the minute plans were finalized, he ended the call, and she threw her phone into her purse.

"Bad news?" Rory asked.

She still couldn't look him in the face. If she saw his lips she'd start thinking about how they felt against hers. She'd remember how he made her forget everything but him. She cleared her throat. "Remember how I said next week we'd shoot the TV commercial in upstate New York?" Rory nodded, and she continued, "Not anymore. Though Devlin approved all the plans, now he wants the commercial shot in Estes Park at the ranch where you work."

Rory's expression darkened and his back straightened as if someone had stuck a broom handle up his shirt. "I'm not shooting the commercial there."

Okay, that was an unexpected reaction. Something didn't fit. "I thought you'd be thrilled to go home."

"I want to keep my personal life and this job separate." A muscle in his jaw twitched, the only evidence of his irritation other than the storm brewing in his eyes. "I'm not sure I can do this job, do things like I did in the interview or the photo shoot, at home with half the town watching."

Her heart twisted for him, and his embarrassment. He always seemed so confident, so comfortable in his skin that she'd never considered posing shirtless might bother him. Guilt swirled through her. She'd been so condescending when they'd met. She'd assumed he understood what doing a national jeans campaign entailed. The thought that he might not realize there would be beefcake shots had never occurred to her.

"How did you plan to keep everyone at home from finding out, when this is a national campaign?"

"When you said that, I thought there'd be ads in magazines like *GQ*. My neighbors don't read that kind of stuff."

"Guess you hadn't considered TV commercials and spots on national morning shows."

"I didn't think I'd be working half-naked, that's for sure," he said in a strained voice. "The news is probably all over town by now. The phone calls and text messages from friends and neighbors will start rolling in soon. I'm going to be a bigger joke than old man Jenkins when he got locked out in the middle of the night in his underwear and had to go to the neighbors to call his wife to let him back in."

"If the interviews and photo shoots bother you so much, then why did you take this job?"

"It's all about the money." Pain flashed in his eyes before he turned away.

"Why do you need the money?" What could drive a proud man like Rory to go against his obviously private nature and accept a nationwide modeling campaign? Nothing but the most desperate of situations. "Do you want to talk about it?"

"I'm fine."

"I'm sorry. I wish there was something I could do. I suggested discussing the shoot location more, but Devlin wasn't open to it."

She didn't dare push Devlin on the issue. In a couple of months it would be time to gear up for the women's spring campaign. If she fumbled things on this one, Devlin wouldn't renew the contract, and she'd be in the same spot she'd been in when she met Rory—facing company layoffs. Unfortunately, if she had to choose between pleasing Devlin and easing Rory's embarrassment, she had to choose the first, but the decision left a bitter taste in her mouth.

"What about if I say I won't do the shoot in Colorado?" he asked at last.

"You'll be in breech of contract. Devlin could sue you, and if you need money, I'm guessing that's not an option."

"You're right about that."

Something dire had forced Rory to take this job. She considered asking him again what was wrong, but it was clear he wasn't interested in confiding in her. So instead she focused on work. "We originally planned on shooting the commercial in a barn. I assume there's one at the ranch." When he nodded, she out pulled her iPhone. "What's the owner's name so I can contact him about shooting the commercial at Twin Creeks?"

"The owner is funny about letting other people use the land. It's been in the family for generations. How about I contact her for you?"

Rory worked for a woman? Interesting, considering his reaction to having Elizabeth as a boss. She frowned. Maybe it was just her he had a problem working for.

"I'd prefer to contact her myself."

"The fact that you're a New York City woman will be a drawback where the owner's concerned."

"You think she'll say no to me because of that?"

"She might, and I don't think you want to risk it."

"You're right."

"I work there. Tell me what you want to spend, and I'll cut the deal for you."

"Are you sure?"

"Trust me. I'll get the job done."

Rory had always been up front with her. If he was upset about something, he told her outright. She'd never pegged him as the kind of man who played games, so why did she have an odd feeling twisting her stomach into one big knot? "Okay, contact the owner for me."

Please don't let me down.

One issue dealt with, the tougher one still to tackle. Their kiss. The mind numbing, all-consuming kiss. "We need to talk about what happened between us after the interview."

"When what happened?"

The cad. Mischief sparkled in his deep brown eyes. He knew exactly what she meant, but he wanted to hear her say the words.

"I want to discuss our kiss."

"It was damn fine."

Heat rushed through her from head to toe as if he'd kissed her again. Why did she have to start feeling something for a man now? And why this man, who was so wrong for her? Shutting off the emotions Rory aroused in her, she said, "I got carried away in the moment. I want to make it clear that there is nothing between us but a professional relationship."

Rory grinned infuriatingly, as if he thought she'd just lied through her teeth. "Sounds to me like you're trying to close the barn door after the horse is long gone."

ELIZABETH HAD MANAGED TO pretty much avoid Rory since their kiss four days ago. The few times he'd caught her on the phone, she'd kept their conversations short and centered on business. She'd insisted she was busy finishing the details for the commercial shoot. Since she preferred to have a cameraman familiar with the West, she needed to hire one from Denver. That took more time than she'd anticipated. She contacted the Chamber of Commerce to get the names of caterers. She worked with the creative team to tweak the commercial copy. After finalizing the plans, she'd met with Devlin so he could approve everything and clear his calendar to join them in Colorado. When Rory asked if she was avoiding him, she hid behind her work.

What a lie. She'd been amazed God didn't strike her down for that whopper.

Everything reminded her of Rory and how marvelous it felt to be in his arms. Now, as the Denver city sights gave way to small towns and farms, she wondered how she could turn off the emotions he'd dredged up in her. Since Devlin still held the remainder of his business over her head, she couldn't let anything get in the way of her job.

"Make sure you drink lots of water and load up on carbs so altitude sickness doesn't hit you," Rory said.

"The joys of being in the mountains. I'd manage to put the unpleasantness of altitude sickness behind me."

"You had trouble with it the last time you were here?"

"Not a bad case, but I was a little sick the entire time."

"You should've told me. We could've spent the night in Denver to let you get acclimated before we went higher into the mountains."

She shook her head. "We don't have time. I've got to get

the details for the commercial hammered out before everyone else arrives tomorrow."

"How many people are we talking about?"

"The agency's art director and copywriter will be there. Devlin will be at the shoot. I've got a cameraman and director from Denver who will be joining us. I think that's about it."

He whistled. "I never knew it took that many people to make a commercial."

"Very few people realize how much time and manpower it takes to produce a one-minute spot. You thought the photo shoot took a long time. Shooting the commercial could take days."

After about an hour, the road grew snakelike. How could she have forgotten how awful the drive up into the mountains was? Must be that she'd suppressed the bad memory.

The road consisted of one curve after another, and they weren't big, slow curves. No, they were those tight, turn-on-a-dime ones that made her clench her teeth and sent her stomach into her throat. Why would anyone want to live up here?

She gulped another swig of water to clear her popping ears, and said a quick prayer that she'd avoid altitude sickness this trip. That is, if she survived the hairpin turns and actually arrived in Estes Park.

Think positive, Elizabeth. You'll make it to the ranch. You'll shoot the commercial, which will be brilliant, and then you'll hightail it out of here, never to return.

Trees zoomed past her line of vision. Her stomach roiled.

"You're looking a little green," Rory commented as he took another sharp curve at what she felt was a ridiculously high speed. "You okay?"

"Could you slow down a bit? The curves and everything zooming past me is not agreeing with my stomach."

"Focus on the horizon instead of what you see out your window. That should help."

His suggestion calmed her stomach a little, but then claustrophobia kicked in. The mountains towered over them no matter where she looked. If she opened her window she swore she could touch the huge trees.

"And people say it's scary to drive in New York? Obviously they've never driven on highways where a mistake could send them plunging off the road to a fiery car crash."

"You're safe with me."

Safe was the last thing she was with him around.

Rory glanced at Lizzie. He'd spent the last four days trying to figure out how he felt about her, and yet he still didn't have a clue. Things had been pretty simple until he'd kissed her. She was his boss and a fun diversion to break up the monotony and tension of the job from hell.

All he knew was things had changed between them when he'd kissed her. Not that little Lizzie would admit it.

That thought kicked him hard in the stomach like an angry mule. Lizzie wasn't half-bad at all. She was pretty as a picture, and he had to admit he enjoyed their verbal sparing. A man had to stay on his toes with her around. He sure liked a woman who had a brain and made him use his.

Too bad she was a city woman who'd made her dislike of his neck of the woods quite clear. And she was his boss to boot.

The woman had created more havoc in his life than a winter blizzard, but she only topped off his current list of problems.

He was going home. Talk about a mess.

"Thanks for handling things with the ranch's owner."

Rory's hands tightened around the steering wheel, his knuckles whitening. No way would he be able to keep his new job a secret. His stomach clenched as he thought about the ribbing his friends and neighbors would give him. Sure, he had a tough skin, but he guessed not thick enough to get through the next few days.

"She's out of town." Thankfully. Dealing with his mother wouldn't be fun. She'd always been able to spot when he was lying. She would confront him about why he'd taken a job he hated, why he'd stepped into the spotlight when he'd spent his life avoiding it. But dealing with that would be easier than explaining Lizzie to his mother.

She'd wonder what was between them, and damned if he knew. Even if he explained he and Lizzie had primarily a professional relationship, that detail wouldn't stop his mother from going into matchmaking mode. Since her cancer diagnosis, she'd started dropping hints about how she wanted to see him "happy and settled down," as she put it.

"She doesn't mind us being there when she's not?"

"She knows I'll watch out for the ranch's interests." Uncomfortable with the conversation, he asked, "What do you think about returning to Colorado?"

"It's very beautiful." Lizzie's eyebrows knitted together. "But I'm not exactly Miss Outdoors."

Yet another reason why he shouldn't be thinking about her the way he had been lately.

With all the worries weighing on him, he wasn't surprised that by the time he parked the Camry in the ranch's driveway he swore he was developing an ulcer. He crawled out and inhaled deeply, filling his lungs with the smells of home. Hay, evergreens and animals. Horses whinnied in the corral. Damn, it felt good to be home. Had he been gone only a few weeks? Felt as if it had been months. If only he was just coming home, and not filming a blasted commercial.

He walked around the car to the trunk, popped it open and hauled out his suitcase, then reached for Lizzie's.

"Leave mine in the trunk. I've got a reservation at the Stanley Hotel."

Maybe that was better. Ever since he'd kissed her, he couldn't keep his mind off the other things they could do together, and worse than that, he wondered what a future would be like with her. He wondered if he could make her happy. He wondered if she cared for him, even though he knew there was no point in thinking those things, not considering where their lives were headed.

The front door squeaked open, cutting off his thoughts and reminding him he needed to oil those hinges.

"Rory, where have you been, and who is that pretty young lady with you?"

His chin dropped to his chest as he realized luck had deserted him. "Mom, I didn't know you were back."

Chapter Ten

Elizabeth stared at the pale, somewhat heavyset woman dressed in jeans, a white blouse and chunky turquoise jewelry standing on the front porch. Rory had her cheekbones and eyes, though her gaze held a weariness Rory's lacked.

"This is your mother?"

He nodded.

The contradictions she'd sensed in him suddenly made sense. He wasn't a simple cowboy. Of course he knew about equity values, negotiations and all kinds of other business dealings. The man continually surprised her. Too bad she didn't like surprises. "You own the ranch?"

"Mom owns the place. I manage the business."

"When I called you a ranch hand, why didn't you correct me?"

"I figured it didn't matter."

"You lied to me." The thought stung.

"No, I didn't. Mom hired me to manage the ranch, and like everyone else around the place, I lend a hand wherever it's needed."

"That's a matter of semantics, and we both know it."

Mrs. McAlister started down the steps toward them. "You stay there, Mom." Rory picked up the suitcases and turned to Elizabeth. "You'll have to stay, now that she's seen you."

"Will you two hurry up? I'm not getting any younger."

Unwilling to offend Rory's mom, Elizabeth headed up the walkway to the sprawling, reddish-brown ranch house. The huge place would house at least four families in Manhattan.

When she reached the porch, she shook hands with Rory's mother. "Hello, Mrs. McAlister, I'm Elizabeth Harrington-Smyth. I'm a management supervisor at the advertising agency Rory's working for."

Beside her, Rory grew very interested in his boots.

Mrs. McAlister's hands went to her hips, and she flashed him a glance similar to one Elizabeth's grandmother gave her when she was particularly annoyed. Not that Rory noticed, with his current boot fascination. "Rory Alan McAlister, what have you been up to? I expect an explanation." Then she turned around and walked into the house.

"You didn't tell your mother about your job with Devlin Designs?"

"Must've slipped my mind."

"Sure, this from the guy who remembered every part of our initial phone conversation."

He shrugged, but said nothing.

"Why didn't you tell your mother?"

He glanced at her feet and her Coach stiletto pumps, which had clumps of dirt stuck to the heels. "I hope you have some sensible shoes."

"I brought flats."

"Are they cute little dainty women's shoes?"

"I wouldn't call them—"

"If they're not work boots or sturdy tennis shoes, they'll be ruined after five minutes of walking in the dirt and grass, and manure if you're not careful."

"I'll be working here, but I won't be *working* here. I'll be fine." After all, how different could this commercial shoot be from the ones she'd done in rural, upstate New York?

"Tell me you brought something other than skirts like

you've got on now. It's pretty on you, and sure shows off your great legs, but it'll be damned hard to work in around here."

He thought she had great legs? Feminine vanity had her blushing and going warm all the way to her toes.

"I've got slacks."

"You should've brought jeans."

That comment erased her glow from his compliment, leaving her irritated at his scolding. She'd packed for this shoot like she would any other, with what she considered practical but fashionable shoes, slacks and blouses. Maybe she wasn't thinking straight, but that didn't mean he had to point out the fact.

She started to fire off an explanation, but then realized how effortlessly Rory had sidetracked her. Again.

The man continually turned her world upside down with steamy looks that got her so hot she thought she'd melt her shoes, or he made her head spin with his word games. Whatever the method, he pulled a fast one when he wanted to change the subject.

Inside the house, a large winding staircase stood to her left. The openness and the sheer size of the space amazed Elizabeth. Glancing right, she spotted an office the size of her living room in New York. She followed Rory into the living room, where his mother sat in a big leather chair beside an equally supersize leather couch. A large picture window filled the one wall with a breathtaking view of the mountains.

While enormous, the home wasn't elaborate. Western, rustic and warm: that's how she would describe it. Thankfully, the place wasn't rustic enough to have dead animal heads tacked up on the walls.

While Elizabeth sank onto the couch, Rory crossed the room, bent down and kissed his mother on the cheek. His large, tanned hand rested on her forearm. "How are you, Momma? You doing okay?"

The tenderness in his voice surprised Elizabeth. He truly

loved his mother. Not like she loved her parents because they were her parents. He loved his mother because he admired her and respected her, and something in his strained features and voice told Elizabeth he was worried about his mom.

"I'm hanging in there." Mrs. McAlister's right hand caressed Rory's stubbled cheek.

The apparent love between them filled the room. Affection so tangible between mother and son that Elizabeth could almost touch it. She looked away.

When she'd last seen her parents, over a year ago, they'd met at a restaurant. There hadn't been any hugs or kisses, merely a mutual exchange of information. Once they'd finished eating, her parents had left for Cairo and she'd gone back to her town house.

Uncomplicated. Unattached. Unemotional. So unlike the scene in front of her.

"Now sit down, and tell me what you've been up to." Mrs. McAlister's gentle voice as she shooed Rory away pulled Elizabeth from her thoughts. "Elizabeth, how did you meet my son?"

She detailed her first trip to Estes Park.

"And now Rory's working for your agency?"

Out of her peripheral vision, Elizabeth glanced at him. From the glower on his face, he wasn't happy that his mother had found out about his moonlighting.

"That right, Mrs. McAlister. Rory's modeling for a client of mine."

"Call me Nannette."

"Rory negotiated an amazing deal with the client. He—"

"No need to bore Mom with the details." Rory pinned Elizabeth with a be-quiet stare. Okay, not only hadn't he told his mother about his job, he didn't want her knowing the details of the deal, either. Why wouldn't he want to tell her how he'd stood up to a Fortune 500 CEO who wanted to low-ball him, and negotiated a sweet contract?

"That was how you got the money I needed, wasn't it?" Nannette's low voice dripped with regret.

Rory nodded. "No big deal."

"You didn't have to do that. We could've found another way."

"Can we discuss this later?"

Elizabeth glanced from mother to son. What was going on? She felt as if she was watching a foreign film without subtitles.

"I'll let it go for now," Nannette said. "But we will talk about this."

"I never doubted we would."

Her parents had shown concern over her being successful and dedicated in her career, but not concern for *her,* as Nannette showed for Rory.

"Tell me you're not modeling underwear," she pleaded as she stared at her son, whose face had suddenly turned beet-red. "That wouldn't be right, and I don't like underwear ads. We all wear underwear and know what it looks like."

Elizabeth opened her mouth to respond, but Rory shook his head, as if to say this, too, would pass.

"Lord knows when the average person wears underwear it doesn't look like it does on a model," Nannette continued. "The ads always do something silly, like showing a man sitting at the breakfast table drinking his morning coffee and reading the paper in his underwear." She paused, then laughed. "Wait a minute. I recall your father doing that a time or two."

"He sure did. Guess that wasn't a good example," Rory teased back.

"How about when they show a woman dancing around the house in her bra and panties. I don't know any woman who does that." Her gazed locked on Elizabeth. "Have you ever done it?"

Elizabeth couldn't contain her smile. She liked this down-to-earth woman with her sharp sense of humor. "I have to admit I never have, and I think those ads are silly, too."

"No son of mine should—"

"I get the point, Mom. You don't have to worry. I'm modeling jeans."

"Thank the good Lord. I can still look Reverend Klockers in the face on Sunday morning," Nannette said, her hand splayed across her chest.

Again Elizabeth laughed. Rory just shook his head, his cheeks still ruddy.

"You're modeling jeans. So that's why you're wearing those fancy britches." Nannette turned to Elizabeth. "No offense, since your client makes those jeans, but they wouldn't last a week here on the ranch. They aren't working jeans."

Note to self. The campaign needs to address the issue that Western people view Devlin's jeans as too fancy.

"That's what I told her, Mom."

"I guess they'd be fine for a night out dancing, though." She flashed Elizabeth an apologetic smile. "This can't be easy for you, Rory. You've never liked being in front of a camera." Nannette turned to her. "When he turned ten he wouldn't let us take his picture. Whenever we brought out a camera he refused to look at us. Once when a friend's mom wanted a picture of the team after they won the Whiz Quiz competition, Rory hid behind another boy."

Guilt over giving him an ultimatum during their first photo shoot sprouted inside Elizabeth.

"Where are my manners? You've been here ten minutes, and had a long trip to boot, and I haven't offered you anything. Can I get you some iced tea or water?"

Elizabeth shook her head. "I need to be going. I want to check into the hotel."

"Nonsense, I won't hear of it." Nannette waved her hand in the air. "That's a waste of hard-earned money when we have plenty of room here."

Elizabeth smiled, realizing where Rory got his frugal nature. "The client is paying for my hotel."

"Doesn't matter. We'd be happy to have you stay here," Nannette said.

"It's not that simple. I have other people joining me tomorrow. Six, in fact, including the CEO of Devlin Designs, and they're all staying at the hotel."

"We're shooting a TV commercial here," Rory interjected.

"Your mother doesn't know about the commercial?" Elizabeth glared at him, trying to control her rising temper. He'd said her being a New York City woman would be a problem for the owner, when in reality he'd talked her into letting him negotiate the right to use the ranch so she wouldn't contact his mother. He'd lied to her twice now. Elizabeth's stomach tightened. What other little surprises waited for her here in Colorado?

"When were you planning on mentioning this?" Nannette stared at him with a look only an irritated mother could deliver.

"I'm sorry, Nannette. Ultimately, this is my fault. I should've seen to the negotiations myself." Elizabeth turned to Rory, struggling not to punch him in the nose for making her look incompetent. "You told me you would clear everything with the ranch's owner. In fact, when I asked you about that very fact on the plane, you told me everything was fine."

Rory ignored her. "Do you trust my decision on this deal, Mom?"

"Of course," she said.

He turned to Elizabeth. "See? Everything's fine. You worry too much."

Nannette laughed. "You're one to talk, young man. That's like the mule calling the donkey stubborn."

"Isn't that the truth." Elizabeth turned to Rory's mom. "I'm sorry that us filming the commercial here has come as a surprise. I'll make sure to keep you updated. I assure you this isn't the way I do business."

"I'd appreciate that. Rory's gotten a little overprotective lately where I'm concerned. He's failed to clue me in on some important details." Exasperation laced Nannette's voice.

"I know what you mean. He's forgotten to tell me a few important things lately, like the fact that his family owns this ranch." She smiled at Nannette. "He can be a bit controlling. Dare I say overbearing?"

The older woman nodded, looked at her son and shook her head.

"You two realize I'm still here, right?"

"When he was little," Nannette said, completely ignoring his comment, "his father and I joked that he would be a great dictator of a small country."

"Thanks for sharing that fact, Mom. Sure makes me look like a fabulous guy." Beside Elizabeth, Rory sat back, his arms crossed over his chest and his jaw clenched. Any minute smoke would roll out of his ears. He liked to tease her, but wasn't so crazy about being on the receiving end.

"Don't get your nose all out of joint. We wouldn't give you such a hard time if we didn't care. Would we, Elizabeth?"

Wait a minute. Now things weren't so funny. Rory's mom thought she cared about him? Major wrong turn. Elizabeth drew a deep breath to slow her racing heart. "I care for Rory like I care for everyone I work with."

That should put things in perspective for Nannette. The last thing Elizabeth needed was a matchmaking mother.

Wise brown eyes focused on her. Elizabeth held her breath as she prayed the woman would buy her fib. Not fib, actually. What she'd said was technically true.

Sure, you care for Rory the same way you care for Chloe, or Jerry, the copywriter. Why don't you try to sell his mom the Brooklyn Bridge while you're at it?

"Rory, take Elizabeth's suitcase upstairs," his mother finally said, breaking the awkward silence.

"I can't stay—"

"Nonsense. If you're shooting a TV commercial here, you might as well coordinate things from the ranch," Nannette said.

Staying here, being able to see Rory anytime, wouldn't be

good. Avoiding him for the last week hadn't helped her put their relationship back on a professional track. No matter how busy she stayed, whenever someone mentioned his name or she saw his picture, her body reminded her how wonderful it felt to be in his arms and have his lips covering hers. Worse was the fact that she'd started wondering what a personal relationship with Rory would be like.

She couldn't stay at Twin Creeks. She needed to put physical distance between them.

"If I cancel my reservation now the company will still have to pay for the room."

"Stephen, the owner, is a friend of mine. He'll overlook that if I say you're staying here."

So much for that escape route. Elizabeth's mind scrambled to find another excuse.

"Stay. I'd like to get to know you better, since you're my son's boss." When Elizabeth opened her mouth to speak, Nannette added with a twinkle in her eyes, "This is my ranch. You need to keep me happy or there won't be any commercial."

That, she realized, settled the issue.

"Rory, get Elizabeth settled upstairs, and join me in the kitchen. You and I need to talk."

Elizabeth resisted the urge to smile. Things could be worse. She could be in Rory's shoes.

AFTER RETRIEVING HER SUITCASE, Rory escorted Lizzie up the winding oak staircase to the second floor. He'd been surprised how well his mom took the news about his latest career endeavor. Of course, with Elizabeth present, how much could she say? Nannette McAlister was a lady through and through, and ladies didn't scold their adult children in public.

Which meant he'd better hold on tight during the storm he'd find in the kitchen. To say his mom wouldn't be pleased that he'd put himself on display for her was like calling the Rocky Mountains a few hills.

"Is your mother always so persuasive?"

"Pretty much." He laughed. His mother could get the entire U.S Congress to vote her way if she put her mind to it. "Dad used to call her the family rock, and said once she'd decided something there was no moving her."

Lizzie chuckled. "I like her."

Before he could respond, Lizzie's cell phone rang. "Hello, Micah," she said as she looked at Rory and rolled her eyes. "Yes, Rory and I are at the ranch." She paused and listened.

Poor Lizzie. Devlin and his micromanaging never let her have a moment's peace. At least he would be at the hotel while she'd be here at the house.

Rory frowned, not sure what he thought about Lizzie staying here. In the short time he'd known her, she'd gotten under his skin, becoming the itch in the middle of his back that he couldn't reach to scratch, and wouldn't go away if he ignored it.

He hadn't found a woman so stimulating, both mentally and physically, in years, probably because he'd shut himself off emotionally since Melissa. But Lizzie had sneaked up on him. Every time he thought he had her figured out, she threw him another curve. As she had downstairs with his mom. The two of them had ribbed him pretty good. He'd given a good show of being upset, but in truth, he'd enjoyed seeing Lizzie have fun. Her pretty blue eyes had sparkled like the little creek out in their eastern pasture when the morning sun hit it. The water looked like it was sprinkled with diamonds.

All those feelings scared him to death.

On the other hand, if she stayed at the ranch, maybe he'd figure out if what he felt for her was real. He opened the guest room door, stepped inside and deposited Lizzie's suitcase by the foot of the bed.

"I plan on familiarizing myself with the ranch as soon as we get off the phone. I'll have any minor changes that need to be made done by the time you arrive tomorrow." Lizzie ended the call. "That man is going to nitpick me to death."

"Don't let him get to you."

"Things are still pretty dicey with Devlin until he renews the agency's other contracts. Until then he can pull the remainder of his business, and I'd be in big trouble."

"You spend a lot of time worrying about losing your job."

"My career is very important to me, and who wants to be unemployed anytime, much less in this economy?"

"Your job isn't who you are, Lizzie."

"I've worked very hard to get where I am. You, on the other hand, don't seem to care about work at all."

"I care. I'm just not obsessed. There are other things that mean more to me, like my family and friends. What else do you have in your life?"

The fact that Lizzie never talked about anything but work hadn't escaped him. She stood before him now, her eyes wide as she tried to figure out how to respond.

"Don't bother. I see the answer in your eyes." How could she live like that? When he stood in front of the pearly gates, Rory figured no one would ask him about his job. They'd ask about the people he loved, and what he'd done for them during his life.

"My life is full and I'm very happy."

He considered asking her who she wanted to convince, him or herself, but decided not to push his luck. He'd need all the luck he could get when he talked to his mother. "I'm off to explain things to Mom."

"Is it true you don't like having your picture taken?"

"I've never liked the spotlight. When I was in Little League the coach wanted me to pitch because I could throw hard and was a lefty. The last thing I wanted was to stand on the mound with everyone's attention focused on me."

"You should have told me."

"Would you have hired me if I had?"

They both knew the answer to that without her answering. Probably not. "But I'd have done things differently at the shoot.

I would've cleared the set of nonessential people. I could've made the experience easier for you."

Rory hooked his thumbs in his front pockets, trying desperately to look as if the conversation hadn't hit a nerve. "What's done is done."

"Is that what bothers Nanette about what you're doing?"

If his mom thought he'd taken the job because he'd wanted to, she'd be all for the idea. What made her mad was that he'd set aside his life to get the money she needed for treatment. And to top it off, he hadn't informed her of his plans.

"What about your dad? Does he know?"

That little arrow shot straight out of the blue and hit him right in the heart, almost knocking him to his knees. "My dad died two years ago."

"I'm sorry. I didn't know. What happened?"

"He and Griff were out fixing fences when Dad had a massive heart attack. By the time Griffin got Dad back to the house and the paramedics arrived, it was too late." Shutting off the painful memories, Rory said, "Mom's upset because our life is ranching. She knows that's all I've ever wanted to do."

Lizzie peered up at him as if she was trying to read his mind. Then she tilted her head slightly to the left. He'd come to realize that meant she was thinking, and that couldn't be good for him. "Is that the only reason she's upset?"

He nodded. "That, and I didn't tell her about it."

"Then why do I feel like there's something that everyone else but me knows?"

Rory kept his features blank, refusing to tell her the truth. No way did he want Lizzie looking at his mom with pity or thinking he couldn't pay for his mother's cancer treatment. "You're seeing things that aren't there. Meet you downstairs at six for dinner."

He turned and rushed out of the room, fearing that if he spent another moment with Lizzie, if she looked at him with those clear blue, understanding eyes, he'd buckle. He'd tell her how weary he was of carrying the family's burdens. He'd tell her how much he longed for a woman to share those worries with him. He'd tell her he wondered if she could be that woman.

Yup, he'd escaped just in time.

AS RORY WALKED into the kitchen, his favorite room, he remembered how it had always sent tempting aromas wafting through the house. Baking bread, apple pies, a good beef roast were among his favorites. During the last few months those smells had been absent.

Today he found his mother seated in a chair at the oak table. A paring knife, ceramic bowl and unpeeled apples sat on the table in front of her. She looked up at him with tears in her eyes. "I'd hoped to make an apple pie, but now I don't seem to have the energy to get it done."

"We'll live without pie." He sank into the chair next to her.

"I hate what this disease has done to our lives."

Then damn it, they'd have pie. At least that one little piece of normalcy. "Is the crust done?"

She nodded and dabbed at her eyes with a tissue.

"You tell me what to do, and we'll get 'er done." He picked up the knife and started peeling apples.

She smiled briefly at his use of Larry the Cable Guy's favorite saying.

"This new treatment's going to change things for the better." From his mouth to God's ears. "What did the doctor say before you left Portland?"

"He said we'd know more when I go back next month. They'll do another CT scan to check the tumor's size, and then I'll have another round of treatment." Her long fingers picked at the fancy side stitching on his jeans. "What do you think of modeling?"

He sliced the apple he'd peeled into the bowl. "Can't say

it's a whole lot of fun, or that it's much of a profession, but it's worth it."

She flashed him a weak smile, and another tear ran down her cheek. "Why didn't you tell me?"

"What would you have said if I had?"

"I'd have told you not to do it."

"Exactly why I didn't say anything." He wiped away her tears with his thumb and picked up another apple. "They're going to pay us good money to shoot the commercial here." Then he told her about the deal he'd negotiated with Devlin.

"I'm glad you're getting to do some business deals. That should make you happy." Nannette covered his hand with hers. "You always put everyone else first."

"It's not that bad, Mom. I'll be done modeling in a couple months."

Then he could put his life back together.

"Now tell me about Elizabeth."

His mom's question hit him right between the eyes, momentarily stunning him. "There's nothing to tell, Mom. She's my boss."

Nannette chuckled. "You can't fool me. The looks you two were throwing each other had nothing to do with work."

He should've known he wouldn't get that half truth past his mother. She always knew when he was lying. "To tell you the truth, I don't really know what's going on. She's a pistol, and she makes me laugh."

"About time you found a woman who can do that. I'd like to have grandchildren while I'm still young enough to enjoy them."

He wished she hadn't said that. Once the words left her mouth, a picture of Lizzie, his child in her arms, sitting in the rocker his grandfather made for his grandmother by the stone fireplace in the living room, flashed in his mind. Surprisingly, the image didn't scare the daylights out of him.

His lack of concern, however, worried him. A lot.

Chapter Eleven

After taking a Claritin to head off her allergies now that she was forced into the great outdoors again, and two ibuprofen for her nagging headache, Elizabeth headed outside to explore the ranch.

As she wandered, she texted Nancy. I'm in the Colorado wilderness. Saying extra prayers. Stay strong.

She wished she could do more than sit with her friend during treatments, or buy her a pretty scarf now that she'd started losing her hair.

As she walked toward the barn across the gravel parking lot, kicking up clouds of dust in her wake, Elizabeth admitted Rory had been right. Her cute little pink Coach flats wouldn't make it out of this shoot alive. She sighed. The things she sacrificed for work.

The thought drew her back to the conversation with Rory. Had she sacrificed too much for work?

Lately, she'd started to think she had. His comment about how life was what happened when you were busy making other plans… Had her ten-year goal kept her from seeing what else her life could be?

After tossing her phone back in her purse, Elizabeth swatted the flies away from her face. Obviously, they hadn't gotten any less persistent since her last visit. Ever since Rory had galloped into her well-ordered life, she'd started questioning where she wanted it to go, and more often wondered if he could fit in somehow.

No, she couldn't go there. She and Rory were too different. Opposites.

She had to remain focused on the commercial. Too many jobs, hers included, still balanced precariously on Devlin's happiness with the jeans campaign.

Clearing her mind, she focused on the scenery around her, studying it in context of the TV commercial. Trees taller than her town house created a canopy around her. Wildflowers decorated the fields. She peered toward the horizon and saw a cluster of animals, elk or deer, munching on grass.

Instead of honking cabs and cell phone chimes, the neighing of horses and the chirping of birds rang in her ears. While that was still a shock, on this visit she could appreciate the beauty around her. She could see how the serenity called to Rory.

Rory. What was she going to do about her growing feelings for him?

Adding him to list of things she needed to sort out, but couldn't deal with now, she grabbed the barn door and pulled, discovering it was locked.

Ever since she'd learned about his camera shyness and his fear of the spotlight, she felt a compassion for him and an admiration she found intoxicating. Neither of which she seemed able to shut off. And there was the kiss they'd shared. What she'd felt when he'd held her and his lips covered hers left her wanting more. Much more.

Stop it, Elizabeth. You're asking for trouble thinking like that.

Assured that the outdoor aspects of the commercial would work and didn't need retooling, she returned to the house. Once inside, her shoes tapped across the hardwood floors as she walked through the living room toward the kitchen in search of Rory's mom. She wanted to ask her to recommend a caterer for tomorrow. Glancing out the windows, Elizabeth marveled at the beauty of the mountains towering outside. They reminded her of Rory—strong, constant and a force to be reckoned with.

In the kitchen she found Nannette at the sink, peering out the window. A view like that would take a lot of the sting out of washing dishes. The enticing smells of roast beef and apple pie wafting in the air made Elizabeth's stomach growl. "Mrs. McAlister, I'm sorry to bother you."

She spun around, a bright smile so like her son's on her face. "You're not bothering me. In fact I'm glad you're here, Elizabeth. I could use a hand."

"I'm not sure I'll be any help." Elizabeth joined her at the sink. "My idea of cooking is reheating leftovers from last night's takeout."

"You've got a pair of hands, so you'll do." Nannette patted her shoulder.

Elizabeth glanced around the open and inviting room. This was a kitchen a family congregated in to share the joys and trials of the day. The kind of room that housed parties with friends.

"A kitchen like this might inspire even me to cook."

"This is my favorite room in the house. When the kids were little, they'd sit at the table doing their homework while I cooked dinner."

She pointed to a spacious alcove off the kitchen with a table for six and large picture windows with another breathtaking view. "I could trust Rory, but I had to keep an eye on Griffin. He'd tell me he'd do his homework in his room, but he'd sneak out to spend time with his friends."

A mother should be there to help with homework and to give kisses for skinned knees, not be traveling around the world digging up the possessions of dead people. The rip in Elizabeth's heart widened.

"But not Rory?"

"He was the opposite extreme. He worked too hard. He'd

spend hours studying for a test. I had to make that boy take breaks."

Elizabeth envisioned a younger Rory studying at the kitchen table, his dark head bent over textbooks. "Has he always been so stubborn and driven?"

When she first met him, she'd never dreamed that would be something they had in common.

Nannette laughed and nodded. "One time when I told him no about something, I can't remember what, he accused me of not listening. I said I'd heard him, but he couldn't believe it. He swore if I listened to him I'd see he was right, and change my mind."

"That certainly sounds like the Rory I know."

"The good thing about that was if someone had a hare-brained idea, Rory told him so, and was confident enough not to get involved."

Elizabeth glanced at the family pictures on the black granite counter and picked up the one of a boy of no more than four on a horse. Rory. No mistaking that strong jaw and determined look. "You have a lovely home." And this house *was* a home.

Her town house would be perfectly decorated, but would it still lack the warmth she felt in every room in the McAlister house? Everyone who walked in the door to her grandmother's tiny house had been welcome and was immediately enveloped in the love. This house felt the same.

"Dinner smells wonderful. I hope you didn't go to any trouble."

"We all have to eat. You can finish the mashed potatoes while I get the roast out and make the gravy."

The thought of a home-cooked meal had Elizabeth's mouth watering, and pulled up memories of Sunday dinners with her grandmother. They'd sit and talk about the upcoming week. Then her grandma would tell her tales of her childhood in Ireland. Elizabeth frowned, remembering how they'd talked about one day visiting there together. Yet another missed opportunity.

Elizabeth walked to the cooktop and stared at the huge pot filled with enough potatoes to feed all of Manhattan, trying to remember what her grandmother had taught her about making mashed potatoes. "Where's the strainer?"

"It's in the cupboard to your left," Nannette said.

"I did warn you that I don't cook, didn't I?"

She smiled. "Mashed potatoes isn't cooking. It's demolition."

"I like your thinking." Elizabeth located the large plastic strainer. After hooking the colander on the faucet, and locating potholders, she grabbed the pot and walked toward the sink.

"What do you think of my son?" Nannette asked.

Elizabeth jerked, sending a handful of potatoes tumbling into the sink. "He's hardworking. The client and I have been very pleased with the work Rory's done so far."

Nannette shook her head as she retrieved the butter and half-and-half from the refrigerator. She placed them on the counter and told Elizabeth where to find the mixer.

While Elizabeth rummaged in the lower cabinet to her left, Nannette continued, "I didn't ask what you thought of my son's work. I'm sure he's doing a fine job. That's how he is. He puts one hundred and ten percent into whatever he does. I wanted to know what you think of Rory as a man."

Elizabeth bumped her head on the counter as she stood, the mixer clutched to her chest. Nannette should warn a girl before asking such a loaded question. Rory made her want to scream one minute and kiss him the next, and the man sure could kiss. The one he'd given her outside the *Wake Up America* studio had nearly singed her eyebrows. "I don't know him well, but he seems very honest and responsible."

"'Honest and responsible'? Poor Rory. That hurts."

Elizabeth turned toward the young woman who floated into the kitchen. She had to be related to Rory; her smile and her good looks were dead giveaways. "I'm Avery, his little sister. He'd say meddling little sister, but don't you believe it."

"A woman could do a lot worse in a man than honest and responsible," Nannette said.

"I agree," Elizabeth echoed.

Avery glanced at her mother. "Mom, have a seat. I'll get dinner on the table."

The two exchanged a look, Avery's filled with concern, her mother's filled with stubbornness.

"I'm fine, dear," Nannette said.

"You sure?"

Something passed between mother and daughter as Elizabeth watched the pair. Something she couldn't identify, though she recognized its importance. First Rory hadn't shared the news about his job with his family, and now this. What was going on?

"Women often make the mistake of wanting to change a man." Nannette retrieved a knife from the butcher block and started slicing the meat. "I loved and accepted your father as he was. If a woman can't do that, all she'll have is a house full of misery."

How different would Elizabeth's life have been if she'd shared similar moments with her mom? One where a mother taught her daughter the things a woman should know. In junior high, Elizabeth had spent a week walking around looking like a clown before a teacher took her aside and showed her how to apply makeup.

"I'm not saying honesty and being responsible are bad things," Avery said as she tossed a hunk of butter and some half-and-half into the potatoes. "But it's not how a man wants a woman to describe him. When women describe Rory usually the first thing they say is how gorgeous he is."

Elizabeth would have to be blind to miss Rory's good looks. Every time she looked at the man, her insides melted like chocolate in a five-year-old's hands. "I noticed how good-looking he is, but we work together. I have a strict don't-mix-business-and-pleasure rule." However, that rule grew harder to follow all the time, but not because of his gorgeous face and rock-hard body. His confidence, his quiet strength, drew her more.

The mixer's whir as Elizabeth mashed the potatoes stalled their conversation.

"You work with Rory?" Avery asked, her eyebrows lowered in confusion. "Are you a horse breeder?"

Nannette saved her from answering. "Elizabeth's in advertising."

"I've been telling Rory for over a year to hire someone to revamp the ranch's advertising. He never wanted to spend the money. How did you get him to dust off the company checkbook?"

Elizabeth swallowed hard and tried to formulate a response that wasn't a massive lie. "I didn't—"

"Dinner's ready. Avery, grab the potatoes, and show Elizabeth into the dining room," Nannette interrupted, once again rescuing Elizabeth from the awkward conversation.

In the dining room, Avery sank into a chair across from Rory. "Elizabeth, you can sit beside Rory. As kids he and Griffin couldn't sit together because they picked on each other, and the next thing we all knew, they were fighting. They still can't sit beside each other, for the same reason."

"You make me sound like I've got the self-control of a ten-year-old," Rory said.

"That's because you and Griff do." Avery flashed her brother a brilliant smile, obviously another McAlister genetic trait. "I was always the good one."

"Talk about rewriting history. I seem to remember Mom and Dad getting called into Principal Johnson's office more than once because you'd stirred up trouble."

"I did not stir up trouble." Avery glanced at Elizabeth. "Mr. Johnson didn't understand my enthusiasm for causes. Instead of seeing me as a forward-thinking youth, he labeled me a troublemaker."

Rory laughed and turned to Elizabeth. "Avery spins a situation almost as well as you do, Lizzie."

"Do you really want to tick both of us off?" Elizabeth said, unable to resist joining in the teasing.

"Elizabeth, I think we can take him." Avery grinned.

"No doubt about it."

He threw his hands in the air. "I surrender, and humbly apologize."

As Elizabeth sat beside him, she understood why she'd felt outclassed when he teased her. An only child, she'd never learned the fine art, while Rory had spent years honing his skills with his siblings.

He leaned closer, his warm breath tickling her skin. "Why didn't you want to sit by me? Were you worried I'd bite? I don't unless I'm invited to."

Her tongue stuck to the roof of her mouth. The man was a first-class flirt. How much of what he did was for show, though, and how much was real? Just for her?

She swallowed hard and thought over the times she'd seen Rory with other women. He been polite, but reserved. Very different than the way he acted with her.

Don't go there. Hoping never led to anything good. It was a direct route to disappointment.

"Stop it. Don't say things like that."

He bent toward her, his lips next to her ear. "If I start nibbling on you, the last thing you'll want me to do is stop."

Elizabeth, her body tingling, her heart hammering as if she'd just finished a Pilates class, glanced at Avery to see if she'd heard his comment.

"Rory, it's rude to whisper when other people are in the room," Avery teased, glancing pointedly between her and Rory, her crystal blue eyes shining with mischief.

"Mind your own business, little sister."

"You're really pushing your luck. I might need to start sharing some of your finer childhood moments. How about the time you dared Griff to—"

"You win!"

"Avery, get Griffin," Nannette said as she entered the room and placed a bowl of asparagus on the table.

"No need, Mom." The smooth drawl, so similar to Rory's, came from the living room.

Elizabeth turned that way. While Rory possessed short dark hair and dark eyes, his brother had shoulder-length, light blond hair and blue eyes. Maybe an inch taller than Rory, he strolled toward the table, a lazy grin on his face. "Hello, pretty lady. I'm Griffin. If you've spent time with big brother here, you're probably about to die of boredom. If you're interested, we could go see what fun we can find around town later."

Another charmer? Obviously the trait was attached to the McAlister Y chromosome. But Griffin left her unmoved. Something in his eyes told her he tossed out compliments like most people tossed pennies into a fountain, and forgot them just as quickly.

Elizabeth had learned early on that some people had personalities they put on like a winter coat when they left the house. Her father was that way. Everyone liked and respected him because he could be counted on to step up and offer assistance to his business associates. Things were very different at home when she'd needed help with her homework. He was either too busy, or was brusque and quick to show his frustration if she didn't immediately grasp a concept.

Elizabeth caught sight of Rory out of the corner of her eye. He wouldn't be that kind of father. He'd be there for his children, and she suspected he would show endless patience, no matter what.

Her stomach tightened. Where had that thought come from? Her hand shook as she reached for her water glass. This bordered on disaster. Her well-constructed wall between work and pleasure had a big hole in it.

"BACK OFF, GRIFF. Elizabeth already has a tour guide if she needs one." Rory stared at his little brother. If he looked in the mirror right now, he'd probably discover his complexion Kermit the Frog green.

When had he started thinking of Lizzie as his? Rewind and change that scene, because it was as dangerous as driving down the mountains during a blinding snowstorm, with seven inches already on the roads.

"So that's the way it is?" Griff taunted.

"That is none of your business."

"Stop it, you two, or take it outside," Nannette snapped. "I don't care which."

Griffin walked to the head of the table, bent and kissed his mother's cheek. "Don't get riled up, Mom. I'm just having a little fun. You know there's nothing I like better than getting a rise out of Rory."

"We have a guest. Pull out your company manners so she doesn't think you were raised in a barn." Nannette took a slice of beef and passed the platter to Griffin, who sat beside his sister.

"Rory, I hear Elizabeth got you to revamp our advertising," Avery blurted out.

"Where'd you get that idea?" he asked as he accepted the platter from her.

"Elizabeth said she worked with you, and Mom said she's in advertising."

Rory clenched his fork. *So it begins.* "We work together, but I'm working for a client of Elizabeth's who makes designer jeans."

"Doing what?"

"I'm the company's jeans spokesman."

Avery laughed so hard tears streamed down her face. When

she finally could speak, she said, "You're modeling jeans? My brother who there are a handful of decent pictures of after the age of ten, is willingly getting in front of a camera? What the heck would make you do that?"

Rory stiffened. Who would've thought he needed to wear armor to dinner? "I couldn't pass up the opportunity."

Elizabeth laughed. "You really think anyone who knows you is going to buy that?"

"Now they won't." He glared at her. "You could've backed me up."

"Backup wouldn't have helped you pull off that whopper," Griff stated.

When faced with unwavering opposition and imminent defeat, a smart man turned to diversion. "What's the plan for tomorrow's TV commercial?"

"The crew should arrive somewhere around noon," Lizzie said, rising to the bait like a hungry trout. "We'll start shooting in the barn if that's all right with you, Nannette."

"That's fine. We have some tours scheduled, but we won't be using the barn."

"You're shooting a TV commercial here?" Avery leaned back in her chair. "I've stepped into the *Twilight Zone*."

"Does feel like that, doesn't it?" Griffin mused.

After helping himself to a hefty pile of mashed potatoes, Rory passed Lizzie the bowl. She deposited a dainty scoop onto her plate.

"You need to load up on carbs." He picked up the bowl of potatoes and held them out to her again.

"I have some, thanks."

"Not near enough." When she didn't take the bowl, he dug out a healthy spoonful and plopped it on her plate.

"I can take care of myself."

"I'm not so sure. Remember what happened when you took charge in Times Square?"

"What happened?" Griff asked.

Rory froze. He'd actually forgotten where they were—the family dinner table with his mother and siblings watching. For a moment all he'd thought of was Lizzie and how she'd had altitude sickness before, and the fact that she wasn't taking care of herself.

He glanced around the table. Three sets of McAlister eyes were trained on him. Avery stared in complete bewilderment. Griff shook his head with pity. His mother tried to hide her smile behind her water glass. "You're looking at me like I've sprouted a second head. What's the deal?"

"Nothing, dear." His mother's smile brightened. "Now what's this about Times Square?"

"Elizabeth stirred up all kinds of trouble."

"I'm not taking all the blame for that mess." She folded her arms over her chest.

"One of you tell us what happened."

"I'm pleading the fifth," Rory said as he stared at his plate. Maybe if he ignored the question, the issue would go away.

"We're not going to stop asking until you tell us," Griff taunted. "You might as well give in."

That worked as well with his family as it usually did, about once every time hell froze over. Rory looked at his mother, hoping to find an ally.

She smiled sweetly at him and said, "Yes, tell us what happened."

He threw his hands in the air and turned to Lizzie. "I give up. You tell 'em."

"Rory was walking around New York City one morning. Some women recognized him from the Times Square billboard, and asked him for his autograph. A crowd of women gathered, then they went a little crazy."

"Crazy I could've handled, but they got grabby." Rory shuddered at the memory. "Talk about assertive women."

Griff laughed. "You never could handle women."

"I'll admit I'm not the master juggler you are. I called Elizabeth for help, but when she arrived she decided I should stick around to sign autographs." Rory turned to her. "Your turn."

"Suddenly everyone was pushing. Coffee went flying. Things were a blur after that." She sipped her water. "The good news was we got an interview with *Wake Up America* out of the mess."

"Wow, I go to Portland and the whole world changes." Avery shook her head.

His sister's comment hit Rory right between the eyes. Lizzie had changed his world.

BEING PART OF A TRUE family dinner had been a new experience for Elizabeth, and she'd enjoyed herself. This was how family meals should be—warm, caring, joking with each other, but with love.

She marveled at the differences in the McAlister siblings' personalities. Rory was the serious one, the manager, the get-it-done guy. Griffin was his polar opposite—carefree, go with the flow, there's plenty of time for work later. The youngest, and only girl, Avery appeared to be the nurturer of the group, and yet could hold her own with her big brothers, trading jibe for jibe.

When she stood and began clearing away the dishes, Elizabeth grabbed her plate and Rory's.

"Put those down," Nannette insisted. "Griffin and Avery are on dish duty. You and Rory head into the living room and talk things over for tomorrow."

After she thanked Nannette for the excellent meal, she and Rory left for the living room. His warm brown eyes gazed at her with concern. "Are you okay? You skipped lunch, but you hardly ate anything at dinner tonight."

"Everything tasted wonderful, but my stomach's a little queasy."

"You need to take it easy, and get a good night's sleep." His thumb brushed her cheek. "You've got dark circles under your eyes."

Her stomach somersaulted. How did he so effortlessly get through her defenses when she least expected it? Desperately needing to get the situation back on a business level, she stepped away. "I need to see the barn before we start taping the commercial. It was locked when I checked earlier. Other than that, we're ready to go for tomorrow."

"You up to it?"

She nodded. Once on the front porch, she glanced skyward. Stars, too many to count, dusted the inky sky like diamonds poured out on black velvet. Rory's cowboy boots rattled across the wood porch as he joined her. "The sky is so beautiful. I can't remember the last time I noticed stars."

"That was one thing that was hard for me when I was in New York." He stood close behind her. While he didn't touch her, his presence enveloped her just the same. "It's so bright and so loud at night. I missed the quiet and the stars."

She laughed. "When I was here before, I had trouble sleeping because it was too quiet. I guess it's all about what you're used to."

Gravel crunched under their feet as they headed from the house to the barn. Rory pulled open one of the large double doors, reached in and turned on the lights. The musty smell of hay tickled Elizabeth's nose as she stepped inside. Thank goodness for Claritin.

Stalls lined each side of the barn, with a wide hall running down the middle. Rory leaned against a wall, his thumbs hooked in his pockets. Casual confidence radiated from him. Sure, he had good looks, but his confidence skyrocketed his appeal. "What's the plan for tomorrow?"

Keep your mind on business.

She needed to impress Devlin on the jeans campaign. Any problems or disappointments on his part put in jeopardy her agency getting him to renew his contract for his other business.

She couldn't afford emotions sidetracking her or clouding her professional judgment. Getting involved with Rory was a train wreck waiting to happen, with her livelihood, not to mention her heart, as likely casualties. Though they could have a lot of fun before the crash.

"You mean what do I have planned if Devlin hasn't had more brainstorms since I talked to him last?"

"You think he'll change something at this stage?"

"Without a second thought. The man's a major pain in the ass. He's even more stubborn than you are."

"The bastard. We ought to string him up."

Laughter bubbled out of her. How long had she kept a lock on her emotions? She'd shut down in so many ways, and she hadn't realized that until Rory barreled into her life. How could she let him be a part of it when he'd ride out as fast as he'd come? She couldn't afford to get attached, because righting her world once he left would then be that much harder. Childhood had taught her that painful truth. Now, eyes wide open, she'd been forced to acknowledge that lesson rather than brush it off.

For years, every time her parents visited, she'd prayed they would stay. She'd pulled out her best manners, trying to show them she wouldn't be any trouble. She'd hinted how amazing it would be for them to be a more conventional family. But they always left, leaving her devastated, lonely and wondering what she'd done wrong.

"It's good to hear you laugh. You should do that more often." Rory pushed away from the wall and strode toward her, his gaze penetrating her defenses. Sparks of electricity raced through her. "You work too hard. You need to have some fun, learn to let go."

He kept advancing.

"This is my job." That was what they were talking about, wasn't it? When he looked at her like she was the only woman in the world, her brain turned to mush. "I have to take it seriously. When I'm more established in my career, than I can worry about the rest of my life."

But did she risk putting her life on hold so long she'd wake up one day and realize she'd waited too long? Was that what she wanted for her life?

Rory stopped in front of her, and for a moment looked as if he might touch her. "None of us knows how much time we have. We can't afford to waste any of it."

"This campaign is crucial. I've got to anticipate Devlin having suggestions," Elizabeth said, desperate to get the conversation on safer ground.

When Rory stepped away, regret flashed in his eyes. "Let's say he realizes the brilliance of your commercial concept and doesn't change a thing. What'll I be doing tomorrow?"

"I know you and your mom say these aren't working jeans, but I think showing you wearing them around the ranch is the best way to convince men that anybody would be comfortable in them." Though she'd turned their conversation to a safer topic, Rory's presence still overwhelmed Elizabeth. "I thought we'd film you riding around the ranch, taking care of your horse and tossing some hay bales around."

"Sounds easy enough."

"Where's your horse?"

Rory motioned for her to follow him. They stopped by a stall across the barn. A beautiful chocolate-colored horse trotted over and shoved its nose under Rory's palm. He stroked the animal's neck. Such beautiful hands and such a gentle touch. Elizabeth bet his hands could do magical things to a woman's body. Her pulse quickened at the sensual images flooding her brain.

Warning bells clanged in her head.

"Don't let Devlin intimidate you," Rory advised. "If he says he's changing something, don't assume it's a done deal. Tell him what you think about the idea."

"He doesn't *intimidate* me. I give him my opinion. He

doesn't listen, and when I can't change his mind, I defer to him because he's the client."

"Looks to me like you roll over and play dead if he pushes you hard."

"He's threatened to pull the rest of his business. The agency's already had one round of layoffs recently. Losing Devlin's business would mean more, with me heading the list because I'm in charge of his account."

Rory smiled. "That's the no-nonsense management supervisor who puts me in my place. Be that person with Devlin. Assertive, but calm and factual. He'll respect that."

"Is that how you see me?" Calm, assertive and factual. Ouch. Not exactly how a woman dreamed of having a sexy man describe her.

Elizabeth held her breath, waiting for his answer, refusing to examine why she cared what Rory thought of her. She wanted him to see her as more than a driven career woman, but what did she want him to see?

A woman he could fall hard for.

Damn that nagging little voice. Especially when it hit the target dead center.

"That's what I see on the surface, the tough, no-nonsense businesswoman. Down deep, I suspect, there's an incredibly sexy woman dying to let loose."

Sexy? The thought burst inside her like fireworks on the Fourth of July, all brilliant, hot and dangerous. Part of her longed to let go and feel something, connect with another human being. Her worst fear was that she'd turn around and become a bitter old lady living alone. Truly alone. No parents. No spouse. No children. Only some distant cousins she hadn't seen or spoken to in years.

"You think you could help that woman get out?" The words escaped before she could snatch them back. Then she realized she wouldn't take them back even if she could.

Rory's callused hands framed her face. "Count on it."

She couldn't think. Blood pounded in her ears as her heart beat at a frantic pace. He was all wrong for her; her head knew that. He wouldn't score a two on her ideal-man checklist, and yet all she could think about was him kissing her. Now. She leaned into him and placed her hands on his cotton shirt. His heart hammered below her palms, matching the frenzied pace of hers.

His lips covered hers, demanding and intoxicating. His hands moved to her hips.

To hell with being responsible. She wrapped her arms around his neck, pulling him closer, until his erection was pressing against her stomach, sending her body into overdrive. His palm covered her breast, kneading and searching. A moan echoed through the barn.

In the back of her mind she heard footsteps, a voice calling Rory's name. But she didn't care.

The next thing she knew, Rory had pried her arms from around his neck and stepped away from her.

Through a haze of frustrated sexual desire, she saw Avery approaching.

"Hey, you two," his sister said, a knowing grin on her face. "Mom has a couple of questions about tomorrow. She sent me to find you."

Elizabeth stared at Avery as the reality of how close she'd come to disaster sank in.

She'd gone beyond breaking one of her cardinal rules— never mix business and pleasure—and had been about to shatter it.

AROUND ONE IN THE MORNING, Elizabeth lay on the ceramic tile bathroom floor, wishing the earth would open up and swallow her. Her head throbbed. The world spun. Her stomach rolled. She hauled herself over the toilet seconds before what little dinner she'd eaten came up.

"Oh, dear, looks like altitude sickness strikes again."

From her position clutching the porcelain god, she discovered Nannette standing beside her.

Elizabeth closed her eyes. Add acute embarrassment to feeling like death warmed over. Now would be an even better time for the earth-swallowing-her-up thing. "I'm fine," she croaked. "I'm sorry I bothered you."

"You didn't wake me. I was up wandering the halls, and saw the light. I don't sleep well lately." Nannette reached over and flushed the toilet.

"I'm sorry."

"No need to apologize. I had three babies within five years. For a while someone was always throwing up. It got so bad once that I didn't feel like I was properly dressed if I wasn't wearing baby barf."

"If I wasn't half-dead, I'd smile."

"Now let's see what I can do for you." Nannette reached into the vanity and pulled out a washcloth. She held it under the faucet, wrung the cloth out, handed it to Elizabeth and then scooted out of the bathroom.

Alone once more, Elizabeth felt her insides pitch. Not again! She fought to keep down what little remained in her stomach. Minutes later a hand started rubbing her back. Focusing on the gentle caress helped her relax. The nausea eased.

A glass of water appeared before her face. Held by a tan, masculine hand. She recognized that hand. It belonged to the man who'd earlier said she was sexy. This scene would certainly change his mind.

"Thank you," she mumbled to Rory. To hell with her embarrassment. She was grateful for the comfort. She accepted the glass, sipped and rinsed out her mouth. Then she took a small drink. All the while his hand rested on her back, offering support and solace. Despite all their differences, all their squabbles, he'd given her more comfort than anyone had in years.

"I'm sorry to be a burden."

"I'm glad you're here instead of at a hotel. There's nothing worse than being sick away from home, except being sick away from home alone. Here we can take care of you."

When was the last time someone had done that? Probably when her grandmother was alive. When she'd gotten the flu last year, Elizabeth had suffered through alone on ibuprofen and chicken soup delivered from the deli down the block.

"What other symptoms do you have?" Concern rang in Rory's voice. "Do we need to head to the emergency room?"

"My head hurts."

"Let me see your fingernails."

Elizabeth raised her hand in his general direction. "Now's a weird time to check my manicure."

He chuckled. "Good. Your mind's clear enough for you to come up with a decent joke. I'm checking to see if your nails are blue, but they're fine. Confusion and blue nails are two symptoms of severe altitude sickness. Is your breathing okay?"

"It's fine."

Rory open the medicine cabinet. Pills rattled in a bottle. A minute later two Advil appeared under her nose.

"Take these. It'll help with your headache."

Elizabeth washed the pills down with the water he'd given her earlier.

"If you're not feeling better tomorrow, I'm taking you to Dr. Harper."

"I have to be better. The crew arrives in the morning, and we're shooting the commercial in the afternoon. All I need is some sleep."

"You need to take this seriously. Altitude sickness can be life threatening."

"Thanks. That makes me feel better." No way would her life end out here in the middle of nowhere. She had plans. Goals to achieve.

There had to be more to life than this. Something longer-lasting. Something that would leave a mark on the world after she turned to dust.

She wanted to be remembered for more than being a hard worker who created ad campaigns to sell jeans and Tug-Ups.

Those thoughts sucker punched her right in the gut.

At least before she met Rory she'd been content. Being with him and his family made her realize how alone she was. How empty her life had become. How could she go back to that?

Super. Altitude sickness mixed with a dose of self-pity. Could the night get any worse?

"You need to take it easy for a couple of days. Altitude sickness leaves someone pretty weak."

She grabbed the toilet, trying to use it for leverage to stand. Immediately, Rory's strong arms wrapped around her, helping her to her feet. For a second she gave in to the urge to rest her head on his arm. His warmth seeped into her. He felt so good. Too good.

She could get very used to having him around.

Now that was something to worry about.

Chapter Twelve

Rory woke the next morning with a crick in his neck from sleeping in the chair in Lizzie's room. He'd been afraid to leave her alone in case her symptoms worsened.

She'd scared the daylights out of him last night. People died from altitude sickness. Granted, not very often, but it happened. Then his fear of losing her had scared him even worse. Just what he needed in his life, one more person to worry about and take care of. But no getting around it, he cared about Lizzie. The question was how much did he care, and what should he do about how he felt?

There couldn't be anything more than a fling between them. Their lives wouldn't allow it. He couldn't see himself in New York any more than Elizabeth could see herself in Colorado, and he wouldn't make the mistake of begging a woman to stay here with him again.

He'd never been big on short-term relationships, but now he was rethinking that policy. A bug bite became all someone thought about when he didn't scratch it. If Rory didn't explore what was between him and Lizzie, he'd wonder about it forever. If he gave in, their relationship would run its course and he could move on. That would work. And if he laid out his expectations before they got involved, no one would get hurt.

We're adults. There's something between us. We both know

we can't have anything permanent, but how about we enjoy each other while it lasts?

Okay, so the laying-it-out-on-the-table speech needed some work.

Lizzie groaned.

"Feeling that good, huh?"

"I feel better than I did last night." Her gaze flicked in his general direction. "Thank you for helping me."

"No problem."

"Please tell me you didn't sleep in that chair all night."

"I planned on staying awhile to make sure you were okay, but then I dozed off."

"You have to look good for the shoot today. You needed your rest."

"Woman, you've got to learn to think about something other than work." He leaned forward and brushed a stray curl off her cheek. "Do you need to bump the shoot back a day?"

"I can't."

Her soft whisper wrapped around him, and for a minute he lost himself in her clear blue eyes.

"I'll have to thank your mother for helping me last night. She's a terrific woman. Your whole family is pretty amazing. You're very lucky."

He didn't miss the wistfulness that slipped into her voice. "They're okay most of the time. What's your family like?"

"There's not much to tell. My parents are archeologists. They travel all over the world."

"Did you go with them as a kid?"

Her lips tightened into a thin line. "I stayed with my grandmother when they were on their digs. When she died my parents gave me the choice of living with my aunt and uncle or going to a boarding school. I chose the boarding school."

Why would a child choose living at a boarding school over moving in with relatives? Then he thought about the situation from a kid's point of view. If her parents didn't want to spend time with her, why would she trust anyone else? The only reason he could think of for a child making that choice was because she wanted to insulate herself from being rejected again.

No wonder Lizzie kept everyone at arm's length. An image of her as she must've been as a child flashed in his mind. Same honey-blond hair, same curiosity filling her eyes. Same keen mind searching for a challenge. How could parents walk away from a gift like that?

"That must've been rough."

She shrugged, but he glimpsed the pain in her eyes. "I survived."

Her quiet strength wormed its way into his heart. The woman had grit. Nothing got the best of her. "I bet you were a terrific kid. They missed out."

She closed down right before his eyes. The vulnerability in her face vanished, as her jaw tipped up.

"I've got to get ready for the shoot." She clutched the blankets to her chin. "You need to leave."

He crawled out of the chair and stood beside her bed. "When you're feeling better, Lizzie, we're going to talk. Things have changed between us."

"No, they haven't. I'm the boss. You're the employee." Her gaze hardened. The closeness they'd shared a minute ago disappeared.

Rory rubbed his thumb along her jawline. "There's been a slow fire burning under us for a while now, and I'm not the only one who feels it."

"I have a rule about never mixing business and pleasure."

"Every rule is meant to be broken." Rory smiled. If Griff heard him say that he'd laugh himself silly. Of the two of them, Rory was the rule follower. He now knew he just hadn't met a rule worth breaking. He intended to smash this one of Lizzie's to pieces.

LATER THAT AFTERNOON, Rory cringed when he walked out of the house to find a good portion of Estes Park's sixty-five hundred residents milling around the ranch. He'd known the juicy news of a commercial being shot at Twin Creeks would whip through town faster than stampeding cattle. He'd told himself he was ready to face everyone, but seeing his neighbors and friends now, he realized nothing could prepare him for everyone he knew turning out to watch him make an ass of himself.

He spotted Joshua Stone and Cade Jacobson, his friends since kindergarten, among the crowd. Damn. Those two wouldn't let an opportunity to harass him pass them by. Rory always gave as good as he got, but today's jokes wouldn't be so easily ignored.

"Mom saw you on *Wake Up America,*" Cade called out. "She said you're on a billboard in New York City. Why would anyone want to see your ugly mug on something that big? Have they gotten complaints about it scaring children?"

Joshua punched Cade in the arm, and the pair laughed. Rory gritted his teeth. They'd tossed insults like this since the moment they'd learned to talk, but today's jibes pricked his skin. Damned if he'd let them see his humiliation, though.

"Your dad still using that picture of you to scare the coyotes off your ranch, Cade?"

"Rory's got you there, Cade. You are damn ugly."

"He's probably all high and mighty now that he's been on national TV, and can't talk to us," Joshua taunted when Rory turned to leave.

"Just look at those fancy jeans he has on," Cade added.

Their loud guffaws bruised his eardrums. "I could pencil you in later, and we could grab a couple of beers at Lonigan's, but now I'm working." Rory tossed this over his shoulder as he started walking toward the barn.

He'd told Lizzie no self-respecting man would wear these blasted jeans. Now he had proof. Knowing he'd been right didn't make wearing them any easier to stomach.

"Working?" Joshua goaded. "Is that what you call it? Doreen sure loved your little striptease on *Wake Up America*."

That zinger dug deep under Rory's skin, drawing blood. He stopped dead and spun around. "You're just jealous because even Doreen hollers for you to put your shirt back on, not take it off." Rory plastered an I-don't-give-a-damn-what-you're-saying look on his face, the one he'd perfected from years of trading insults with his mouthy younger brother.

Cade pulled out his iPhone and pointed the thing at Rory. "How about you strike a pose for us? We can print the pictures and sell them on eBay. If you'd autograph them, that is."

His patience stretched thin, he was about ready to punch his buddies in the nose, lifelong friends or not, when Lizzie materialized at his side.

"I'm sorry, gentlemen. You can't take pictures, since this is a commercial shoot. You're welcome to stay in the parking lot, but this area is closed to the public." She placed her hand on Rory's forearm. Despite the weariness in her eyes and her pale complexion, she emitted her customary take-charge attitude. "I'm sorry to drag you away from your friends, but we need to get started."

"Those two should send you flowers," Rory muttered as he and Elizabeth walked away.

"I know. You were about to take a swing at them."

He froze. "How'd you know?"

"Intuition. I figured you needed an out. I've situated a spot for you and the stylist in a far corner of the barn. No one can see you from there. I'm off to check the lightning."

Her concern for him, for his embarrassment, and her attempt to help him salvage his pride, wrapped around his heart and squeezed.

Minutes later, as he sat having his makeup done—no way would he ever get used to that—he couldn't get his thoughts off Lizzie and how she'd sensed what he needed and rescued him. That had always been *his* role in the family. Damned if being on the receiving end didn't feel good.

His gaze sought her out where she was talking to the cameraman. She looked like she'd been dragged behind a truck for a mile or two. He noticed she didn't have any water on hand. He needed to remind her to keep hydrated, and he needed to get her a chair, too. She appeared ready to topple over any minute.

"Why didn't you tell Joshua and Cade why you're doing this?" Avery asked as she stopped beside him.

"Yeah, that would be better, telling them I can't afford to pay for Mom's medical treatment."

"Everyone knows how expensive health care is these days." His sister put her hands on her hips. "They'd want to help. The whole town would. You're not Superman, so quit trying to pretend you are."

"We don't need handouts."

"Pride is a good thing, to a point."

"I can handle our finances."

"I know that." Avery nodded in the direction of Rory's friends. "They know that. I know how hard this job is for you. You're not a spotlight kind of guy like Griff is."

"If I hadn't found a way to pay for Mom's treatment, I'd ask for help. But since I've got this wonderful gig, I don't need to."

"What can I do to help you?"

"Keep an eye on Elizabeth. She had a rough night with altitude sickness."

"I'd be happy to, but won't you be with her all day?"

"I won't be able to make sure she takes care of herself while I'm working." Rory glanced toward Lizzie. "She doesn't have any water, and she needs a chair. She can't stand all day. Plus this client of hers is a real pain in the ass. If he gets too irritating, distract him so she can get the commercial done."

Avery smiled like she had when they were younger and she knew a secret. He braced for her latest revelation.

"Wow. You've got it bad."

He scoffed. "I'm just concerned about her welfare. She's my boss."

"I saw how you two looked at each other last night in the barn, so no way am I buying that fish story." Avery rubbed his arm. "I'm thrilled. It's about time you found someone. You worry too much about everyone else. You need someone to worry about you. I like her, especially since she doesn't bow down to you."

"It can't go anywhere between us."

"You don't know that."

"Yes, I do. She lives in New York. I live here. My idea of a relationship isn't a long-distance one. I'm not big on phone sex."

"You never know what fate has planned." Avery smiled and nodded toward Elizabeth. "Don't wait too long before you let her know you're interested. You're not getting any younger."

"You're acting like I'll be getting my AARP card any day now."

Elizabeth called his name and motioned for him to join her and Devlin. "Gotta go," Rory said to Avery. "I'm on the clock."

As Elizabeth watched Rory stroll toward her, she remembered how she'd woken to find him sitting beside her bed. His concern for her had been touching, but then he'd spoiled everything by talking about their relationship.

The man could be so impossible, but so unexpectedly kindhearted, and oh so delicious. She should be mad at him for wanting to talk about how their relationship had changed, but how could she when he was right? Things were different between them, but she wasn't yet sure what she wanted to do about the fact.

"We're starting with you in the barn," she said when Rory joined her and Devlin. "We'll shoot you getting your horse ready, then ushering it out of the barn. Then we'll film you riding around the ranch."

"How's that going to fit in with our real-man slogan?" Devlin asked.

Elizabeth bit her lip. They'd been on the set for only thirty minutes, and the man had already maxed her out with questions. Every one of which sent of rockets of pain through her throbbing head. Soon she'd be popping Advil like they were Altoids. How many ibuprofen could a person take without risking overdosing?

"I emailed you a copy of the voice-over dialogue," she said with as much politeness as she could muster.

"I haven't had the chance to read it," Devlin admitted.

Why would he take time out of his schedule to read the copy himself? Not when he could take time he'd set aside for the shoot and have her explain it to him.

Sure, he could waste *her* time. "The voice-over will talk about Rory's day, then end with the line, 'no matter where your day takes you, Devlin's men's jeans can handle the job.'"

Devlin nodded in approval.

"Rory," Elizabeth began, "go about your business like you would any day. The camera's here to film what you're doing. It's not like the still photo shoot, where I wanted you to look at the camera."

"Got it."

A few minutes after the filming started, Avery materialized beside Elizabeth with a canvas collapsible chair and a refillable water bottle.

"Sit," she whispered in her ear. "You won't make it through the day if you don't."

Realizing the truth in what she said, Elizabeth gratefully sank into the chair as Avery shoved the water bottle into her hand. Smiling, Elizabeth mouthed *thank you* and sipped the water.

Luckily, she felt better than when she'd woken up. This morning when she'd swung her legs to the floor to get out of bed, the small motion set her world spinning. It took a few minutes for the dizziness to pass, and twice as long as usual for her to shower and dress. Now if she could just make it through the shoot today without collapsing, she'd be happy.

"I'm not sure about Rory's shirt," Devlin began.

Add *or killing her client* to her list.

What problem could he have with a simple beige, button-down shirt?

"It's one of your shirts." Elizabeth smiled. What she wouldn't give for a muzzle. Hey, maybe one of those bridle things scattered around the barn would work.

"I like the shirt. Rory looks super in it," Avery interjected. "The light cream color accentuates his complexion and his brown eyes without detracting from the jeans."

Elizabeth smiled, thankful for the unexpected support. "You should be in advertising. That was very well put."

"I think he'd look better in a darker color," Devlin insisted, and crossed his arms over his chest.

"Let's go with what he has on," Elizabeth said with as much assertiveness as she could muster, considering her throbbing head. "We'll review the film before dinner, and if you're not happy with what you see, we'll try a darker shirt tomorrow."

Devlin thought for a moment, and at one point seemed as if he might argue, but finally nodded, momentarily pacified.

One bullet dodged. How many other details would he question before the day was over?

Maybe she'd get lucky and he'd be struck mute. She smiled at the thought. A girl could dream.

Turning her attention back to the commercial, she watched Rory. His biceps rippled as he tossed the saddle onto the horse's back. Definitely eye candy, but she'd come to realize how much more there was to him. She admired his honesty and his work ethic. Though he didn't exactly admire the advertising business, he gave this job all he had.

He looked so comfortable, so at ease here at the ranch. Had she ever been this comfortable in her own skin?

No.

She longed for the contentment, the peace she sensed in Rory. She longed for a family like his. She longed for him.

Damn. She couldn't fall for Rory. Talk about a doomed relationship.

"Cut," the director called out.

"Great job, Rory," Elizabeth said, shaken over her recent thoughts. "We're going to do it again so we can get closer shots of the jeans and your face." She turned to the cameraman. "How's that sound to you?"

"I'm not sure about this horse," Devlin said before he could answer.

The man had to be kidding. He had problems with the horse she'd cast? Wasn't the animal horsey enough?

No way would both she and Devlin survive the day.

"The animal's fine. It's Rory's horse. That adds a familiarity, a relationship element, to the commercial," Elizabeth snapped. "You need to let me do my job."

"Wait a minute," Devlin countered.

She'd opened her mouth to tell him to keep his insane questions, comments and ideas to himself when Avery placed a hand on his arm. "Mr. Devlin," she said as she flashed him a dazzling smile.

"Call me Micah." He turned his attention to Avery, and if his mouth hadn't been closed, his tongue would've scraped the floor. Not that Elizabeth blamed him. No woman in a plain pink tee, khaki shorts and no makeup should look as good as Avery did.

"Micah, how about I show you some of our other horses?" She linked her arm through his. "Then if you aren't happy with Blaze—that's Rory's horse's name—you'll know what other animals you have to choose from."

"That's an excellent idea," Elizabeth said.

As she stood there, slightly stunned at the masterful way Avery managed Devlin, the pair strolled off. Of course, it helped when a woman looked like a cover model. After a couple steps, Avery looked over her shoulder, smiled and winked.

Elizabeth smiled back. Avery had just saved Devlin's life, because a minute more and she'd have strangled the man.

Rory's family amazed her, accepting and helping her more than her parents ever had, making her soul ache, knowing she'd have to leave.

Forcing back ridiculous, pointless tears, Elizabeth turned to the crew. "Okay, everyone, let's get those close-ups shot."

Later, when they broke for dinner, she turned to Avery. "Thanks for running interference with Devlin."

"Is he always that big a pain?"

"Pretty much."

"How do you stand working with him? I'd tell him to take a hike, and hope he got lost on the trail."

"I wish I could, but his company is responsible for over half my agency's business. Otherwise I'd have told him that a long time ago."

"I hope all your clients aren't like that."

"They all have their moments, but he's the worst." Elizabeth thought back over the last couple years since Rayzor Sharp Media had landed Devlin's account. Had she truly been happy? *Hell, no.* The answer burst through her. She hadn't realized until now, but the joy had been missing in her work lately. Every day it became harder and harder to get up, knowing what she'd find when she went into the office—messages from Devlin questioning something she'd done, or informing her of his latest brainstorm. If she didn't have him to deal with, then invariably, another client had a problem needing her attention.

Was this how she wanted to spend the rest of her life, working with pain-in-the-ass clients?

Rory had turned her world upside down. Now his family added to the emotional chaos churning inside her, making her want what she couldn't have. She'd been way happier, or at least thought she was, before she'd met him.

She wished she could turn back the clock, because ignorance was definitely bliss.

PEOPLE HAD NO IDEA how hard and monotonous modeling was. Rory had spent the day doing the same thing over and over until he thought he'd go crazy. If people knew what the job really entailed they'd never say it was a glamorous profession.

At eight, Elizabeth finally wrapped up the shoot and told everyone they'd start back at six tomorrow.

Rory stood in a stall brushing Blaze after he'd unsaddled the poor horse for the last of countless times today. The animal snorted and shook his head.

"I know, fella, you don't get why I saddled you so much and we never went anywhere. Welcome to the wonderful world of modeling."

The horse snorted again.

"That's what I think. It's a real blast."

"Commercial filming days are long," Lizzie said as she came up behind him. "Unfortunately, it'll be another long day tomorrow, too."

"We're tough. We can take it." He patted Blaze's neck, then turned to Lizzie. He'd been so busy concentrating on following directions during the shoot, he hadn't gotten a chance to really look at her. While some color had returned to her cheeks and she seemed steadier on her feet, she still had dark circles under her eyes. "You hold up okay today? I'm tired, so you must be exhausted."

Terrific line. Real romantic. Tell the woman you've got the hots for that she looks tired.

"I made it through relatively unscathed, thanks to Avery. She had Devlin following her around like a little lapdog."

"She has a way of doing that with men."

"I can't imagine why. Just because she's tall, blonde and gorgeous. Do you think she'd consider modeling?"

Rory shook his head. "Avery's in vet school."

"Wow, she's got brains, too. God was way too generous with your sister."

He reached out and tucked a strand of hair that had escaped from Lizzie's ponytail behind her ear. "You're every bit as pretty and as smart as she is."

A pink blush spread across her cheeks. "I wasn't fishing for a compliment."

"I didn't say you were." He moved closer, wanting to explore the attraction boiling between them. Since he'd met Lizzie he'd been thinking about things he hadn't in years—marriage, kids, building a house of his own on his patch of land.

Blaze whinnied and shoved his muzzle into Rory's back. Glancing over his shoulder, he said, "Can't stand not being the center of attention, can you, boy?"

"He's a beautiful horse."

Blaze stepped toward Lizzie.

"He's a sucker for a pretty woman."

She reached out as if she wanted to touch the horse, but pulled back at the last minute. Rory moved behind her, took her hand in his and placed her palm against Blaze's neck.

Her pretty flowery scent filled his senses. Hell, everything about her filled his senses. Her fast, shallow breathing echoed in his ears. Her tight little butt brushed his thighs. Electricity from the simple contact shot through him, threatening to incinerate him from the inside out, and bringing him immediately to half staff.

Lizzie stroked Blaze's neck. The image of her stroking Rory in an entirely different manner materialized in his mind.

"He loves being scratched behind the ears."

She glanced over her shoulder. "How about you?"

"Honey, you can touch me any way you want."

He bent down and kissed the sensitive spot where her neck

met her shoulders. Her moan filled his ears. She leaned back into him, and her hands clutched his thighs.

While everyone thought making love to a woman in a barn was romantic, it wasn't. Hay got in all kinds of awkward places, and the stuff itched like crazy. He wanted more for his first time with Lizzie. She deserved more.

"Your room or mine?"

Chapter Thirteen

"Rory, Elizabeth, you still in here?" Devlin shouted from somewhere in the barn.

Elizabeth flinched. Rory rested his forehead against hers.

"Damn. Talk about bad timing," he said, his voice and body tight. "If we ignore him maybe he'll leave."

"No way. He'll search the place until he finds us." Elizabeth pulled away and straightened her clothes. "We're in here, Micah."

Rory picked up the brush and moved to the opposite side of the stall, behind his horse. She smiled when she caught sight of the evidence of his desire.

"Micah, I thought you'd left," she said, when he entered the stall. "Rory and I were going over the day's events, and discussing the plans for tomorrow."

While her body still hummed from Rory's touch, she clamped down on those emotions, trying desperately to slip back into business mode.

"I need to talk to you both before I leave for the hotel," Devlin said.

"I'm off the clock," Rory barked. "We can talk first thing in the morning."

"I agree," Elizabeth stated. "It's been a long day for all of us."

"What I want to discuss affects tomorrow's shoot."

When Elizabeth glanced at Rory, he looked as if steam would roll out his ears any minute. "Doesn't matter. I'll talk to you in the morning," he insisted.

"You and I can talk in the house," she told Devlin as she headed out of the stall.

"I need to talk to *both* of you."

The CEO's words halted her. She spun around and glanced back at Rory with a please-help-me-out-here look.

"You've got five minutes. No more," Rory conceded as he stormed out of the stall toward the barn door, Elizabeth and Devlin scurrying after him.

A couple minutes later Rory ushered them into the living room.

"I'm getting some water. Either of you want some?" He looked directly at Elizabeth.

"I'm fine," she mumbled as she sank into the nearest arm-chair.

"Me, too," Devlin echoed from his spot on the couch.

When Rory returned with two glasses of water, he handed one to Elizabeth. "You need to keep hydrated because of the altitude sickness."

Devlin turned toward her. "You're sick?"

"I'm fine. I've got a mild case of altitude sickness."

"It's more than a mild case," Rory said as he glared at Devlin. "You're lucky she's so dedicated. She should've spent the day in bed."

"I've always admired Elizabeth's dedication. That was one of the reasons I signed with Rayzor Sharp Media." Devlin cleared his throat. "Which brings me to the opportunity I have for you two and the agency. Based on response to the billboard and the *Wake Up America* interview, indications are this campaign will be a real winner. Because of that, I want to expand it to include other aspects of our men's line. We've recently added boxers and boxer briefs to our product line."

Elizabeth glanced at Rory. He sat with arms crossed, jaw clenched, staring at Devlin.

Rushing to prevent Rory from exploding like Mount Saint Helen's, she said, "Right now we need to concentrate on shooting this commercial. Once we're back in New York we can discuss expanding the campaign."

"Elizabeth, I want you to develop a campaign to showcase our other products, especially our underwear line," Devlin continued, a big smile on his face. He was apparently unaware of the storm brewing around him. "The average man is the perfect market and, Rory, I want you to be the product spokesperson for all our men's products."

"I'll model pants, shirts, shoes, even ties, but no way in hell am I modeling underwear."

Devlin's smiled faded, replaced with a scowl. "Let's discuss this."

"There's nothing to discuss, because I'm not changing my mind." Rory stood and stalked out of the living room.

Elizabeth wished she could escape, too, but she had to pacify Devlin.

Rory's outright refusal put her in an awkward spot. Again. Smack-dab in the middle between him and the client. She wasn't cut out to be a peacekeeper. How did UN ambassadors do this kind of thing for a living and not end up in a rubber room?

With the jeans campaign under way, they'd already started their branding strategy. A new model would confuse the consumer.

"You need to change his mind," Devlin said to her.

All she wanted to do was crawl into bed and pray the whole mess evaporated by the time she woke up.

"If there's one thing I've learned working with Rory, it's that there's no talking him into anything."

"Since his contract covers only the jeans campaign, I'm

willing to make it financially worthwhile for his participation in this new endeavor."

"He's a proud, private man. Modeling underwear crosses a line for him."

"Convince him otherwise."

"Let me do some thinking tonight. There may be a way we can get Rory to advertise the product without him having to be photographed wearing them."

"My assistant is sending boxers Fed-Ex. I want to get photos of Rory in the underwear here at his ranch. Maybe we could shoot another commercial if you wrap this first one up quickly."

Sure, she could whip up commercial shoot details on twelve hours notice. She'd have to be David Copperfield to pull off that trick.

And what did the guy think they'd do? Put Rory in a pair of boxers and video him riding his horse around his ranch? That'd be classy.

Elizabeth dug her fingers into the leather couch arms and struggled to control her rising temper. "Micah, creating a commercial isn't something we want to do on the fly. It takes careful thought and a lot of planning to be a successful part of a coordinated campaign. We're smarter to finish this commercial and work out a new campaign strategy to include other items from your product line once we're in New York."

As she struggled to decide how to deal with this latest harebrained idea, Devlin continued. "How difficult could shooting an underwear commercial be? We put Rory in the boxers, and film the commercial in his bedroom and his bathroom, showing him getting ready for a day working around his ranch."

Yeah, that's all there was to it. Elizabeth closed her eyes and counted to ten, then counted to twenty. When she opened them she still wanted to strangle Devlin. Maybe if she explained the situation the jury would see the crime as justifiable homicide. She inhaled deeply and pushed aside her murderous thoughts.

Calm and factual. That's how Rory said she should deal with Devlin. "It may seem that simple, but it's not."

"Elizabeth, there you are."

She looked up and discovered Avery standing in the doorway.

A savior. Thank you, Lord.

Rory's sister glided across the room and stopped in front of Devlin. "I'm sorry to interrupt." She flashed him a contrite look.

"No need to apologize," Devlin answered, his eyes glued to Avery's beautiful face.

Elizabeth bit her lip to keep from grinning. Forgive her? What man wouldn't be thrilled that a goddess like her was interrupting?

"I've been looking all over for Elizabeth," Avery continued sweetly. "Mom sent me to find her. She has a question about tomorrow's shooting schedule. I'm afraid I'll have to steal her for a while."

"That's no problem." Devlin turned to Elizabeth. "I'll give you until tomorrow afternoon to get that idea to me. Then we go with mine."

Yippee, a last minute reprieve from the warden.

Elizabeth nodded, stood and followed Avery out of the room. Once in the kitchen and out of Devlin's hearing, she said, "What's your mom's question?"

"She doesn't have one. I was rescuing you."

"Once again you're a lifesaver, but how did you know I needed help?"

"When I saw Rory a minute ago, he said if you and Devlin were still meeting, I was to get you out of there."

Elizabeth smiled. Rory playing her knight in shining armor? Who would've thought?

"Where is he? I need to thank him."

"He's in his office, and for the record, he's the one who asked me to keep an eye on you today."

A minute later Elizabeth stood in front of Rory's office door, suddenly unsure of herself. She'd come to thank him for sending Avery to rescue her, but found herself wanting more.

Somewhere along the way she'd quit caring about their differences. Even if the relationship couldn't last, she wanted to feel his strong arms around her. It had been so long since she'd cared about a man. She wanted him holding her close, exploring her body. She wanted *him*.

That was enough for right now.

With courage, hope and longing filling her, she knocked on the door. When he called out for her to enter, she opened it and walked in, having decided to seduce her employee. To hell with not mixing business and pleasure.

RORY LOOKED UP FROM the pile of invoices on his desk to see Lizzie walking into his office. He'd been amazed how well she'd held up today, considering the rough night she'd had. In fact, if he hadn't known she was sick, he wasn't sure he'd even noticed anything different in her work performance today. She'd been focused, demanding. The same little slave-driving perfectionist.

So much grit and strength in such a compact package.

One he'd like to spend a lifetime unwrapping.

Whoa, back up that train.

Even if he asked her, which he wouldn't, Lizzie wouldn't give up her career in New York to start all over in Colorado.

"Thanks for sending Avery to rescue me." She glided across the room toward him, a look he'd never seen before—hot, intense, determined—filling her eyes. Something more scorching than a raging Colorado brush fire blasted through him. He leaned back in his chair. If any other woman but Lizzie looked at him like that he'd think she was about to seduce him, but Lizzie had a clear-cut hands-off policy regarding coworkers.

She stopped in front of him and placed her dainty hands on his knees.

Gently, she pushed his legs apart and stepped between them. She licked her lips and looked at him as if he were the last piece of prize-winning apple pie at the county fair. Trying to wrangle in his raging desire, he grabbed a deep breath before he dared open his mouth. "Lizzie, you need to step back."

She smiled, but didn't move. "I'm bothering you?"

"That's an understatement, and if you don't put some distance between us right now, we're gonna end up a lot closer."

"I don't have a problem with that."

Every nerve in his system went on high alert. Before they continued, he had to make sure she understood where things were going. "If you don't take your pretty little hands off me, in about ten seconds you'll find yourself under me on that couch over there, my hands exploring every inch of your beautiful body."

She licked her lips and her palms moved to his thighs. The fire raging in him scorched another ten acres.

"What about your not mixing business and pleasure rule?" His hollow voice bounced off the office walls.

"I've decided you're right. Every rule is meant to be broken."

"That's all I needed to hear." Rory pulled her into his arms and his mouth captured hers. His body kicked into high gear. Passion gnawed at him.

Her fingers clutched his chest as she leaned into him. He deepened his kiss. His tongue mated with hers as his hand covered her breast, caressing and exploring. Her passionate moan thrilled him.

When Lizzie ground her pelvis against his erection, he nearly exploded. "Damn. I never should've moved back home."

"What are you talking about?" Her husky whisper fanned his heated skin.

"One, you deserve a bed, not to be tumbled on a couch. Two, my mother lives in this house."

"I want you. Now." Lizzie reached for the zipper on his jeans. The scrape of metal filled the room.

He sucked in a breath as her hand slid inside his waistband, gently caressing his heated flesh. Sweat broke out on his forehead as he fought to not explode right then and there.

"I don't mind being quiet, and beds are overrated."

Chapter Fourteen

Elizabeth's cell phone alarm blasted her awake at four. Rory, curled around her, his incredibly talented hand cupping her breast, slept through the noise.

As she shut off her alarm, she felt her face flame with embarrassment. She'd made love with Rory in his office. Then they'd sneaked up to his room. Propriety might have ruled her life with an iron fist before, but not once Rory wrapped his arms around her. When she broke the rules, she broke them with a passion. A passion she'd never felt before.

At least she'd had the presence of mind to set an alarm for an early escape. The last thing she wanted was someone in Rory's family seeing her slinking out of his room in the morning.

She spent a few precious moments watching him, remembering how she'd discovered the man possessed unbelievable stamina and skill in bed. He'd also been surprisingly tender the second time they made love. He'd explored every inch of her as if he'd been trying to file the details away.

What had she done? Sure, she had amazing memories to hold on to now, but how would she ever go back to New York and leave him here in Colorado?

She leaned over and kissed his forehead, longing to fight reality's rude advance. Then she sighed and slid out of bed.

"Where you going?"

She snatched up her blouse and threw on the garment.

"Don't you think it's a little late for modesty?" He flashed her that million-dollar smile, and her heart melted. She'd see that smile in her dreams forever.

"You've got a point, but I've got to go."

"The sun's not even up. Come back to bed."

"I don't want anyone to see me coming out of your room."

Resignation replaced desire in his warm brown eyes. "I'll stand guard."

He tossed off the covers and stood. Her resolve wavered at the sight of him.

She had to get out of here fast, before she threw away common sense and her heart. His future lay here in Colorado. Hers resided in New York.

He joined her at the door and kissed her tenderly. She knew she needed to say something, but the right words eluded her. Finally she forced out, "I'll see you at work in a little while."

How lame was that?

"This is the first time I've looked forward to coming to work since I left the ranch."

Rory opened the bedroom door and scanned the hallway. "All clear."

After giving him a quick kiss, she scooted out of his room.

Her reality had spiraled so out of control since meeting Rory, and yet she now realized her life needed mixing up. While she'd thought herself happy, she'd been barely content, more numb than anything. Rory had showed her what life could be if she opened up to the possibilities. No going back now, but the scarier question was if she went back, what would she be going back to?

ALL DURING THE SHOOT, Elizabeth struggled to keep her focus on work. She couldn't help melting every time Rory sent her a steamy glance. She hoped no one noticed. How would she leave him tomorrow after what had happened between them last night?

They finished shooting the commercial just before dinner. Both she and Devlin survived, thanks again to Avery's distractions. Once the crew had packed up and left for the hotel, Elizabeth asked Devlin to join her in the McAlister living room. He sank onto the caramel-colored couch while Elizabeth sat in the chair to his right and resisted the urge to wring her hands.

"I hope you're as happy with what we've accomplished here as I am," she said as an icebreaker.

"Rory is the perfect spokesperson for our new markets."

"Speaking of Rory, I've come up with an idea that I think will please both of you regarding the underwear campaign." She cleared her throat, kept thinking positive and sent out good energy. Maybe it would work, provided the good vibes bored through Devlin's thick skull and actually hit brain cells. Hey, stranger things had happened. Look at Elton John and Eminem performing together at the Grammys.

"Imagine Rory answering the ranch house door. Standing on the other side is a gorgeous woman. Dangling from her index finger is a pair of Devlin Designs' boxers. I haven't completely worked out the dialogue, but she could say something like, 'You left these at my place.' We could also do a shot with Rory in bed. He's leaning against the headboard. The sheets are pooled at his waist."

Elizabeth paused and reminded herself to remain assertive and focused. "Another idea I had has a woman coming out of the bathroom. She walks toward Rory, wearing his boxers. She smiles and asks if they look as good on her as they do on him."

For the first time since she'd started talking, Elizabeth glanced at Devlin.

He wasn't doing cartwheels over her ideas, but his thoughtful gaze told her he was considering them. Better results than she'd expected.

His contemplation and openmindedness lasted only another minute before he frowned. So much for visualizing the outcome. She was definitely asking for a refund on the positive thinking course she'd taken.

"Your idea won't work because it pulls the focus off Rory. With him wearing the product the focus remains clearly on him and underwear."

"If the camera remains on him, I think the viewer will stay focused on Rory as well, and with him in bed shirtless, what woman would take her eyes off his gorgeous body?"

"Surely you can convince him to change his mind." Devlin paused, gazing pointedly at her. The look in his eyes soured her stomach. "You two seem like you've become close."

Damn. Devlin had noticed. Elizabeth swallowed hard. *Remain calm. Don't show any reaction to what he said, because no way could he know exactly what had happened between them.*

Sure, she and Rory had acted differently at the shoot today, but the changes were subtle. He didn't question her directions as often. A couple times she'd asked what he thought about how she envisioned a shot. A few times she'd caught him staring at her with a look that would melt the polar cap. But Devlin couldn't know *how* close she and Rory had actually become.

"Rory and I have settled into a comfortable working relationship."

"Good. That should help when you talk to him."

She clenched her hands together so tightly her fingers went numb. How could this man even suggest she use her relationship to strong-arm Rory into changing his mind? Devlin proposing she do so left her needing a hot shower to scrub off the scum.

Then realization dawned. He expected that because in the past she'd compromised her principles to keep his business. Every time he threatened to agency shop, she knuckled under, so why wouldn't he expect her to do so now?

"You don't know Rory if you think anyone can talk him into doing something."

As if on cue, Devlin's eyes narrowed and he folded his arms across his chest. "I can take the remainder of my business elsewhere."

She was so tired of him holding that over her head. She thought about her town house—the first real home she'd had since her grandmother died—along with its mortgage payment. She'd saved enough to survive a couple months, but to avoid losing her home she couldn't be out of work longer than that.

Her career and her town house were all she had. Her chest tightened from the weight of her decision. What a lousy choice. Her pride and principles, or keeping her home and everything else she'd worked for.

No, that wasn't true. If she lost her job and her town house, she'd still have her self-respect and her dignity.

She was done with Devlin's ultimatums. No longer would she compromise her principles and give up bits of her soul to keep his business. She'd hit her breaking point.

"I won't try to talk Rory into doing something he doesn't want to do. If you want his arm twisted, you'll have to do it yourself." She straightened, vowing to not let him bully her. "I do value your business, and I've worked very hard for your company, but I won't play on his trust and respect for me, or our personal relationship."

"I'll be contacting Ms. Rayzor about ending our association."

"I'm sorry to hear that." Elizabeth stood, shook Devlin's hand and lied through her teeth saying it had been a pleasure working with him. Then she turned and walked away.

But now that the worst thing she could imagine, losing the Devlin Designs account and probably her job, had happened, the incapacitating panic she'd anticipated didn't come.

An unexpected sense of freedom flooded her system as the world opened up to her. She could pursue any of the career options she'd dreamed of! But what did she want, deep down in a corner of her heart? Realization burst inside her. She wanted to be in charge of her life, not at the mercy of pain-in-the-ass clients she hadn't chosen to work for.

Now all she needed to do was find a way to turn that dream into an income before she lost her town house, her shirt and her mind.

RORY SAT IN THE KITCHEN with his mother. Last night, after Lizzie had fallen asleep, he'd mentally replayed his discussion with Devlin. Then his mind fixated on the ranch's financial state. He'd started modeling because he needed money. That hadn't changed. In fact, he needed more, because his mom had told him she'd require more treatments than the doctor originally thought. Unable to sleep, Rory had gone to his office and crunched the numbers.

He'd examined the ranch's expenses and income. He'd pulled up his mother's medical treatment and prescription costs. Then he added in Avery's vet school tuition. He ran the numbers three times, each time hoping for a different result.

No matter how he worked them, without added income he came up in the red. Bright red.

As he sat at the kitchen table now, with memories of his happy childhood swirling around him, he knew what he had to do.

"Devlin wants me to model underwear." He tossed out the statement, hoping his mother wouldn't immediately string him up before he had the chance to explain.

"Absolutely not. Under no circumstances." She glared at him. "Am I making myself clear?"

Yup, expected reaction right on cue. "The contract I signed only covers jeans. Devlin will have to negotiate a new one to cover other products. To do the underwear, I'd make him pay some serious money."

"It's not worth it." His mother rubbed his arm, her initial

storm subsided. "It's not worth your pride. I know how much you've sacrificed already."

Sure, doing so was at the expense of his pride, but he could take the hit. "Lizzie's always telling me I have more than my fair share of pride." His joke fell flat. Instead of coaxing a smile from his mom, he received another glare. "I could earn enough for your treatment, anything else you need, and Avery's tuition."

His mother pulled her hand away from his arm. "I won't let you humiliate yourself. We'll be fine."

Rory rubbed his neck, fatigue suddenly overtaking him.

"No, Mom, we won't." His mother, the eternal optimist. His words twisted his gut, because he hated being so blunt, but she needed to know the truth. "I ran the numbers last night. With all the expenses, unless we increase our income, we're running in the red."

"Then we'll cash in some stocks or annuities."

"What we've got left for stocks won't put a dent in your medical bills. Dad and Griff's bills from Dad's first heart attack and the accident wiped out our savings." Now that he'd actually started talking about their financial state, he couldn't stop the flow of words. "We'd started recovering, but then Dad had another heart attack. I sold almost all the stocks and cashed in whatever I could to pay for those medical bills and his funeral. There's nothing to draw from, Mom. Our income is down because people aren't vacationing as much or for as long as they once did. People don't have the disposable income to buy our horses or to board them here at the ranch. We need more money."

"He's right, Mom," Griff said. Entering the kitchen, he went straight for the refrigerator, where he grabbed a can of Pepsi, popped the top and took a long drink. Then he joined them at the table, tilting his chair back.

His mother turned to him, tapping a manicured nail on the oak tabletop—a screaming indication of her irritation. "You knew we didn't have money for my treatment, Griffin Ryan, and you didn't tell me?"

Griff's chair hit the floor with a loud thunk. "He threatened to beat the crap out of me if I told anyone, and let's face it, he's bigger than you are."

"You should have told me," their mother said in a soft, iron-filled voice.

Griff paled, and Rory knew if he looked in the mirror right now, he'd find his own complexion a similar light color. As children, he and Griff had learned that the quieter their mom became, the greater her anger. They might outweigh her and tower over her now, but they both knew to take cover when Momma got mad, and she was red-hot furious at the moment.

Her piercing brown eyes focused on Rory. So much for his short reprieve. "You took this job to pay for my treatment without telling me we didn't have the money to pay for it. This is a family problem, and we'll deal with it as a family. I will not be kept in the dark about finances. Is that clear?"

Both he and Griff mumbled, "Yes, ma'am," as if they were ten years old again.

Nannette turned to Griff. "They want Rory to model underwear, and he's considering the idea. Tell Rory a man with an MBA from Harvard Business School can't do that." His mom's voice broke and tears filled her eyes when she looked back at Rory. "You worked too hard in school to do this. Surely we can find some other way."

"We've been trying." Rory's heart ached for the truth he'd forced his mother to face.

"I could help. You shouldn't have kept this from me. I'm not some child that needs to be protected."

"Mom, take it easy. It's not good for you to get so upset," Rory pleaded. "I didn't tell you about this because I knew you'd overreact."

"You're right about that."

"Rory was doing what he thought was best, Mom. Cut him some slack," Griff added.

Nannette stood, her face flushed. She was obviously madder than he'd ever seen her. This much stress couldn't be good for her system, which was already taxed to the limit, coping with her latest treatment.

She needed to calm down. As Rory rose, his mother swayed. He and Griff raced around the table toward her. Rory caught her before she hit the floor. "Call 911, Griff."

"Already am!" his brother yelled.

"What's wrong?" Avery rushed into the kitchen. "Oh, God, no. Mom. Is she unconscious?"

"Go meet the paramedics, Avery." Rory's voice cracked. He swallowed hard. "Hang in there, Mom. Don't leave us."

Chapter Fifteen

Avery tore through the house toward the front door, almost knocking Elizabeth over on the way through the living room.

"Avery, what's wrong?"

"Mom collapsed. We've called 911. I've got to meet the paramedics."

"Where is she?"

"The kitchen."

"Stay with your mom. I'll meet the paramedics."

Avery nodded and ran back toward the kitchen. Elizabeth raced out of the house onto the front porch, with what she'd overheard when she went to talk to Rory swirling in her head. Treatment? Nannette appeared healthy, but obviously she had some condition requiring medical care. Apparently expensive enough to drive Rory to model to earn the money. Elizabeth took a deep breath as the answer to why Rory had changed his mind about her offer sank in. He needed the money to pay for his mother's medical bills.

He'd put aside his pride, his privacy, his dreams, to help his mom.

What a man. What an incredibly magnificent man. A man who'd sacrifice whatever he had to because of his love for another person.

And Elizabeth had derided him over being interested in nothing but money. Of course the job had been all about the money for him. He could have so easily put her in her place by telling her he needed cash for his mother's treatment. Elizabeth had been a fool, and she owed him an apology.

Then what his mother had said sank in. *Tell Rory a man with an MBA from Harvard Business School can't do that.*

Shame washed over her as she recalled various conversations she'd had with Rory. She'd lectured him on the ripple effect business downturns had on the overall economy.

She'd met him on a horse ranch and assumed he wasn't college-educated. She'd misjudged him and looked down on him because of her assumptions.

At any time he could've put her in her place by throwing his Harvard education in her face, but he hadn't. Tears filled her eyes. She, on the other hand, had repeatedly tossed her education and business sense right in his. He'd shown his true character in every interaction with her.

Her heart melted. No woman could ask for a better man.

She'd been able to deny how much she loved Rory before. Now there was no escaping the fact. She'd finally fallen head over heels in love, despite trying to guard against the fickle emotion. She'd found a man she wanted to spend her life with, only to discover herself unworthy of him.

As she stared into the darkness enveloping her, she prayed the paramedics would arrive in time. She prayed that Nannette's collapse had been caused by something other than whatever disease she was fighting. Nannette had to be okay. She was such an incredible woman. Her family loved her so much. What would they do without her?

Flashing red and blue lights colored the early evening sky, and sirens blasted through the quiet as the ambulance roared toward the house.

"She's this way," Elizabeth said to the paramedics once they arrived. She stared at them. Both men, tall and athletic, one blond and one dark haired, could be on the cover of any magazine.

"Is Mrs. McAlister conscious?"

"I don't know. Avery didn't say."

"Have they contacted her oncologist?" the dark-haired paramedic asked as he flung open a panel on the ambulance and pulled out a duffel bag.

"Nannette has cancer?" No, not that fantastic, spunky woman.

He grabbed a portable machine from another compartment. "She's got a rare kind of inoperable brain tumor. She's undergoing experimental treatment in Portland."

Elizabeth's heart dropped. Experimental treatment meant every conventional one doctors tried had failed. Experimental treatment meant a last-ditch effort to stop the cancer. Experimental treatment meant desperation.

She regretted every time she'd pushed Rory to do things he wasn't comfortable with. She'd accused him of not taking the job seriously. No wonder he'd been so incensed when she'd renegotiated his deal.

Money was literally a matter of life and death for his mother.

The rear ambulance doors clanged shut. The second paramedic joined them with a gurney. Elizabeth raced up the walkway, threw open the front door and stepped aside for the EMTs to enter.

When she'd followed them to the kitchen her eyes filled with tears. Avery sat on the ceramic tile floor, her mother's head in her lap, tears streaming down her beautiful face. Griffin sat beside them, worry etched on his classic features. Nannette's arm was splayed across her son's lap.

Rory paced the room, his eyes dark and his face drawn, a cell phone held to his ear. "The paramedics are here. What do I need to tell them about her treatment?" He nodded toward the dark-haired EMT. "Glad it's you, Brandon."

"We'll take care of her." Rory's siblings moved away as

Brandon knelt beside Nannette. "Mrs. McAlister, can you tell me if you're hurt anywhere?"

She weakly shook her head.

The second paramedic attached disks to various spots on Nannette's shoulders and one to her chest. He then clipped on wires and connected them to the portable machine. Next, he slipped a clip onto her index finger and took her blood pressure. After studying the machine, he said, "Your vitals seem strong. Blood pressure's a little high, though."

A second later Rory approached and handed his phone to Brandon. "It's Mom's oncologist in Portland. He wants to talk to you."

Stark panic shone in Rory's eyes when he joined Elizabeth. She glanced at Griffin and Avery, who stood huddled together a few feet away from their mother. Similar worry etched their faces.

Rory's voice wavered. "I refuse to lose Mom, too."

Elizabeth wrapped her arms around his waist. He leaned against her, just the littlest bit. Not enough for anyone else to notice, but close enough that his pain radiated through her.

"I hate feeling helpless," he murmured, as they watched Brandon start an IV on Nannette.

That done, the medic walked toward them. Rory stiffened and moved away from her, all the vulnerability she'd seen in his eyes earlier, gone.

"She's stable, Rory, so that's a good sign." Brandon returned his BlackBerry. "Her oncologist said as long as she's stable, the best thing to do is get her to the hospital. He's calling the E.R. doctor to update him on Nannette's treatment."

"Thanks, Brandon."

"We'll meet you at the hospital."

Rory joined his mother, knelt beside her and kissed her forehead before the EMTs loaded her on the gurney. "If you wanted a little attention, Mom, all you had to do was ask."

"There are some things you need to know—" Nannette began weakly.

Avery's sniffles echoed in the room.

"Tell me tomorrow," Rory said, and then turned to his friend. "Take good care of her."

"You got it." Brandon walked to the head of the gurney. "Now, Mrs. McAlister, I don't want to hear any complaints about my driving. I'm a more responsible driver now than when Rory and I were in high school."

After his mother and the EMTs left, Rory looked at Griffin. "We should have two cars at the hospital. You and Avery ride together, and I'll drive there in my truck."

"See you at the hospital," Griffin called as he and Avery left the kitchen.

Once they were alone, Elizabeth stared at Rory. His hands shook as he pulled his keys out of his jeans pocket. She joined him and held out her hand. "Give me the keys."

"I've got to go to the hospital. Will you be all right here?"

"You're in no shape to drive."

"I'm fine."

"No, you're not." She caressed his cheek with her hand. "Let me help you."

He handed her his keys, fatigue and worry causing his broad shoulders to slump. "You drive. I'll navigate."

As she and Rory made their way through Estes Park's darkened streets toward the hospital, she longed to tell him that everything would be okay, that his mom would be fine. She glanced at him in the passenger seat, and her heart froze. The strongest, most capable man she'd ever known had tears in his eyes.

"When was your mom diagnosed with cancer?"

"Around a year after my dad died." Rory's voice broke. "I don't know how she did it—going through chemo while still dealing with dad's death. Sheer force of will, I guess."

"She's an amazing woman." Elizabeth's hands tightened around the steering wheel. "That's why you changed your mind about modeling, isn't it? You needed the money to pay for her treatment."

"Who told you?"

"I overheard part of your family powwow."

"I wouldn't have pegged you as an eavesdropper."

"I'm not. I was coming to talk to you. Devlin wanted me to talk you into doing the underwear gig."

"I'm not changing my mind."

"I'm not asking you to." Elizabeth pulled into the hospital parking lot and followed the signs directing her to the emergency room entrance. "I told Devlin if he wanted your arm twisted, he'd have to do the job himself."

"I may have to give in."

"You can't compromise. Not when you're so adamantly opposed to it."

"If you heard the discussion earlier, then you know that without additional income, the ranch is running in the red."

Elizabeth pulled into a parking place. "What's your advertising plan?"

"There's the website, and we've got brochures in the hotels and the tourist bureau."

"Maybe that's part of your cash flow problem."

"Now's not a good time for me to talk business."

"Sorry, old habits are hard to break." Elizabeth turned off the engine and handed Rory his keys. Then she crawled out of the truck. She couldn't help him with his business issues right now, but she could help him in other ways. "Who do I need to call about your mother? Does she have family other than you kids who need to be notified? How about a pastor?"

"I haven't even thought about that."

Elizabeth reached into her purse and pulled out her iPhone. "Tell me who needs to be called."

Rory rattled off names as they strode toward the emergency room entrance, and she compiled a list. The hospital's giant motion sensor door swooshed open as they approached. Griffin and Avery stood to one side of the reception area, Avery's shoulders shaking with the force of her emotion as she cried in her brother's arms.

"Has something happened to Mom?" Rory asked, his voice filled with panic.

Avery stopped crying and gazed at them through red, swollen eyes. "We haven't heard anything yet."

Deep worry lines etched Griffin's forehead. "I'm hoping no news is good news."

"I'll find out what's going on." Rory stalked toward the reception window. "Lucy, how's Mom doing?"

The nurse behind the desk smiled at him. "They're running tests now, but she's conscious and coherent. In fact, she's giving Dr. Greer a tough time. She keeps insisting she's fine and wants to go home. He says no matter what, she's spending the night."

Rory laughed, but not his normal full-bodied laugh. This one held a brittle quality. "Sounds like Mom."

"She's one tough lady." Elizabeth joined him and rubbed his arm. "That will help her get through this."

"You need to register her," Lucy said.

As Rory reached in his back pocket for his wallet, another nurse rushed out a door to the left. "Dr. Greer wants to talk to all of you. He needs to do a CT scan, but your mother says she hates 'those damn things' because they're noisy and claustrophobic."

"You two go," Rory said to his siblings. "I'll join you once I get Mom registered."

"We've got your mother's information on file." Lucy nodded toward Elizabeth. "We'll get her paperwork taken care of. You can sign any necessary forms later."

Elizabeth held out her hand. "If you give me your phone, after I'm done with that, I'll call the people we talked about."

Rory leaned toward her, kissed her on the cheek and handed her his BlackBerry. "Remind me to thank you later."

After he and the others left, Elizabeth turned to Lucy. "Would you point me in the direction of registration?"

"I'll take you there," Lucy said as she came around her desk. "That boy has always carried more than his fair share of the family burden. He needs a woman who's strong enough to take some of that weight off his shoulders."

"Rory and I work together. I'm his boss," Elizabeth said, hoping to clear up the receptionist's misconception before it spread through the town. "We're not involved."

No. They were just sleeping together, but only for now. And she loved him more than she'd ever imagined possible.

Lucy laughed. "Honey, you're not fooling anyone. My guess is not even yourself."

No kidding.

Fifteen minutes later, Elizabeth made her way to the waiting room and sat with Avery and Griffin. "I've called Reverend Klockers. He's on his way. I've also called your uncle. He'll take care of everything at the ranch. He figured that was the best way he could help. If you want him to come to the hospital, you're to call him. I checked Rory's BlackBerry. There are tours scheduled for tomorrow." She glanced at Griffin. "Do I need to reschedule them?"

"Uncle David and I can see to them."

Elizabeth checked off the item on the to-do list she'd compiled while registering Nannette.

Avery linked her arm through Elizabeth's. A fresh batch of tears pooled in her eyes. "Mom has been through so much, and now this. What if the tumor's growing? What if the experimental treatment doesn't work? What if—"

"Avery, don't even think those things. Take a deep breath." Elizabeth clasped her hand, then breathed deeply, encouraging the younger woman to breathe with her. Once Avery appeared more under control, Elizabeth said, "Show me where the cafeteria is. I could use some coffee."

Rory's sister hesitated.

"I could use a cup myself," Griffin stated. "Go on. I'll talk with Uncle David about the tours while you're gone."

"You'll call if..." Avery stopped, unable to continue. She bit her lip.

Griffin patted her arm. "Mom's tough. She's going to be okay."

"We won't be gone long." Elizabeth stood and gently coaxed Avery to her feet. "I hear you're in vet school. What's that like?"

As they left the waiting room, Elizabeth glanced over her shoulder at Griffin. Phone to his ear, he mouthed the words *thank you.*

RORY LOOKED UP to find Lizzie and Avery entering the waiting room, their hands filled with coffee cups. He'd joined Griff a few minutes ago with a list of things to take care of, only to discover Lizzie had seen to most of them. Without his asking. Without him having to lead her through things step by step. All his life he'd been the one everyone looked to during a crisis. He figured that was part of the oldest-child job description, but sometimes, like tonight, the role weighed him down.

Accepting a coffee cup from Lizzie, he smiled. What a woman. She could hold her own in the business world. She could laugh with him and trade zingers point for point. Now she'd taken care of things he hadn't even realized needed to be done, like checking tomorrow's tour schedule.

He could get used to having her around. Someone who worried about him every once in a while. Someone he could count on. Someone he could love and grow old with.

Realization hit him as hard as running headfirst into a ten-point elk.

He'd fallen in love with his little Lizzie.

Now the question was what the hell should he do about it?

One thing he knew, he wouldn't beg her to stay. He'd made that mistake before.

"How's your mom?" Elizabeth asked as she sank into the chair beside him.

He twined his fingers with hers, sending little ripples of heat through her. "Dr. Greer thinks she collapsed because of fatigue and stress, but he's doing more tests to be sure. When he's got all the results, he'll fax them to Mom's oncologist in Portland, and they'll talk over the results."

"If I'd known she was sick, I would've talked Devlin out of doing the commercial at Twin Creeks." Tears pooled in Elizabeth's eyes. When she sniffled a bit, Rory traced circles on her palm with his thumb.

His actions confused her. He'd never given any indication that he wanted a permanent relationship with her, yet here he was, turning to her for comfort. Was that all this was, him needing comfort and her being convenient?

Please, let him think we had more than that.

"Don't beat yourself up over it. If anyone's to blame it's me. I should've checked to make sure she was still in Portland."

Lizzie squeezed his hand. "I guess we're both at fault."

"Stop it, you two. It doesn't matter, and feeling guilty won't help. We need to focus our energy on helping Mom," Avery stated, her gaze and her voice filled with censure.

Both brothers stared wide-eyed at their sister. Rory nodded. "You're right. You always manage to keep things in perspective, Avery." He smiled weakly. "Mom's stable. We don't know how long she'll be in the hospital. All of you need to go home and get some sleep."

Both Griff and Avery shook their heads.

"What if Mom's situation changes?" Avery blurted out, then her eyes widened in horror, as if her saying the words could bring about the event.

"Us being here won't keep that from happening." Rory released Elizabeth's hand. "I'll take the night shift. Then tomorrow, when I'm sleeping, you can stay here with Mom, Avery, while Griffin takes Elizabeth to the airport."

Rory's words, said so calmly and without regret, crushed Elizabeth. Her heart shriveled and then she went numb.

What had she expected when she'd thrown herself at Rory? That he would declare his undying love for her and beg her to stay, because he couldn't bear for her to leave him?

Obviously unaware of the turmoil churning inside her, Griff turned to her. "What time's your flight?"

"It's at one-twenty, but you don't have to take me. I turned in my rental car when we arrived, but I can rent another one."

She sat there wishing Rory would ask her to stay. She longed to tell him how much she loved him and that she wanted to spend the rest of her life with him, but she couldn't. Right now she had nothing to offer him, and he had enough problems. She refused to add to his burdens.

And he would worry about her. He was that kind of man. One who shouldered his family's problems and worked to ease their situation. He'd feel partly responsible for her unemployment because it resulted from her unwillingness to talk him into modeling underwear. Not that she believed that, but Rory would feel obligated to her, and she'd never be sure if he was with her out of love or not.

Relationships started when one person's life lay in ruins never went well.

"I'll take you." Griffin's voice broke through her thoughts. "We can drop Avery off here in the morning and then head to Denver."

Flashing what she hoped was a no-my-heart-isn't-in-pieces smile at Griffin, she said, "That would be perfect."

Chapter Sixteen

Rory stared out one of the hospital's huge picture windows, watching for Griff and Avery. When he'd received Griff's text saying they were on the way, Rory had left their mom sleeping in her room, and headed for the hospital entrance. A minute later Griff's dark blue Chevy truck pulled into the parking lot.

When Rory saw Lizzie, as well as his brother and sister, crawl out of the truck, his heart fell. He'd hoped she wouldn't come to the hospital today. Letting her go last night had been hard enough. Seeing her now was like pouring rubbing alcohol on an open wound. When he'd tossed out the comment about Griff taking her to the airport, he'd held his breath. He'd prayed she would say she couldn't bear to leave him.

When she didn't, he unsuccessfully tried to force the words asking her to stay past the lump in his throat. He'd traveled that road before, begging a woman to stay, to love him, and he'd crashed and burned. A smart man never made the same mistake twice.

The hospital door whooshed open and Rory smiled, trying to pretend his stomach wasn't full of knots. His gaze remained locked on his siblings as he updated them on their mom's condition. If he looked at Lizzie, he feared he'd beg her to stay in Colorado. With him. Forever.

The hospital door slid open behind them, ushering in a gust

of fresh Colorado air and Micah Devlin. Lizzie stiffened and moved away slightly as he approached.

Rory glanced from one to the other. What was up there?

When Devlin reached them, his adoring gaze locked on to Avery. "How's your mother? When I checked out this morning the front desk manager told me she collapsed last night."

Not happy with Devlin's interest in his baby sister, Rory said, "We're waiting for test results. Then Dr. Greer and Mom's oncologist in Portland will go over everything in a phone conference."

Devlin reluctantly turned toward Rory. "If it would help, I'll send the company jet to Portland and fly your mother's oncologist here. Or if they'd have better treatment for her in Portland, I can fly her there."

For a minute Rory stood there regrouping. Talk about a shot out of the blue. Once he recovered from his shock over Devlin's unexpected offer, he murmured, "Why would you do that? If it's to get me to do the underwear campaign, it won't work."

"My grandmother had cancer."

It made sense now. He belonged to the cancer-patient's-family club. That explained why Devlin made the offer, but did Rory want to accept? He'd given up bits and pieces of his pride over the last months. How much more could he lose before the well was tapped out?

He had to draw the line somewhere. "Thanks for the offer, but we're doing fine."

Lizzie turned to Griff and whispered something.

"What did you say, Elizabeth?" Rory scowled at his brother. "What's going on?"

"I asked Griff for his keys." Lizzie shifted awkwardly. "I thought I'd wait in the car while all of you talked."

Was she that eager to get away from him? Rory stared into her eyes, trying to determine what she was thinking.

Please. Tell me you want to stay. That you can't bear to walk out of my life.

She held out her hand to Griffin.

Avery glanced between Rory and Elizabeth as if she wanted to say something, or hit him. Rory couldn't tell which. Griffin tossed him a what-do-you-want-me-to-do-bro look.

Rory wouldn't beg her to stay. He couldn't. If he asked Lizzie to remain in Colorado with him and she turned him down, how could he survive her rejection? Letting her go was safer. "Griff, take Elizabeth to the airport so she doesn't miss her flight."

A WEEK LATER, Rory sat in his office, staring at the mountains, still reeling from Lizzie's departure. He'd felt connected to her in a way he'd never imagined possible, especially after she'd gotten him through the scare with his mother. The love he felt for her made what he'd shared with Melissa seem like a childhood crush.

He'd thought about calling Lizzie, but she hadn't given him any indication she wanted anything to do with him. He'd hoped when he mentioned her going to the airport, she'd say something about wanting to stay, but apparently, they'd scratched each other's itches and now the fling was over.

At least he hadn't begged her to stay. This way, while he hurt like hell, he still had his pride. Granted, that wasn't much, but as his dad used to say, it was better than a kick in the teeth.

How could he have thought he could have a brief affair with Lizzie? He wasn't a love 'em and leave 'em guy like Griff. Rory wanted—hell, needed—that emotional connection, and the minute he'd touched Lizzie, deep inside he'd known he never wanted to let her go. He'd been a fool. Making love to her hadn't gotten Lizzie out of his system. Instead he'd fallen even more in love with her.

His cell phone rang. Hoping to find Lizzie on the line, he glanced at the caller ID. Disappointment crashed over him when he instead saw Devlin's name. Rory had to stop wishing she'd call. A man could handle only so many letdowns before he became a masochist.

He answered the phone, and again thanked Devlin for offering the use of the corporate jet.

"Avery said she and your mom fly to Portland once a month. If you email me the treatment dates, I'd be happy to send the jet for them."

While Rory's pride wanted him to say he could get his mother and sister to Portland, his financial common sense won out. Eliminating airfare costs would save a chunk of change, and he'd come to realize there was no shame in accepting help. "Thanks. I'll send you the dates."

"Now on a business note, I need to inform you of a change I've made," Devlin said, his voice oddly strained. "I've signed with another agency for the rest of the men's campaign."

"You fired Elizabeth?"

"I parted company with her agency on the rest of my business. Her firm will still be handling the advertising for our men's jeans."

Rory had taken business speak 101 at Harvard. No way was he buying Devlin's whitewashed version. "What happened to Elizabeth when you pulled the rest of your business?"

"There's no point to this line of discussion."

"There is to me."

"I heard she was part of the layoffs Rayzor Sharp Media recently went through."

Elizabeth had lost her job, the thing that meant the most to her, because she wouldn't talk him into modeling underwear. She was a single woman trying to support herself in New York. Not an easy thing to do considering the cost of living. Damned if he'd let her lose her job because she wouldn't twist his arm.

"I've signed with Harms and Finn," Devlin continued, after an awkward silence. "The new management supervisor will contact you regarding advertising plans for other products in our line."

"Hold on there. I don't have a contract for anything other than jeans." Rory smiled. Turnabout wasn't only fair play, it felt damned good.

"I'm sure we can come to an understanding regarding further ventures."

"Not if it doesn't include Elizabeth."

"This is business. Don't let your feelings for a woman cloud your judgment."

Rory's hand tightened around his cell phone. "I'll say this once. My personal life is none of your concern."

"I didn't mean to offend you. I should have said that we can make this a profitable business relationship for both of us."

"I'm not modeling underwear. Not even if hell freezes over."

"We'll put that on the back burner."

Devlin's twinge of desperation raced across the phone lines. Rory smiled. Being in the driver's seat was the only way to travel.

"The new management supervisor and I will fly to Estes Park," Devlin continued. "We can discuss plans for the rest of the clothing line."

"I don't work with anyone but Elizabeth."

"I'm sure once you meet Matthew, you'll like him."

"It's not a matter of liking the guy or not." Rory leaned back in his desk chair and stretched his legs out. "Elizabeth earned my trust and respect. If the deal doesn't include her, forget it."

"That's not the best decision for my company."

"You aren't the only one who has news to share. The billboard and *Wake Up America* interview created quite a buzz. I've had other major men's clothing companies contact me about acting as a spokesman for their lines," Rory bluffed.

"We have an exclusive contract."

"For jeans." Rory paused. "I bet any one of those companies would be willing to hire Elizabeth, too."

"We agreed that you'd be Devlin Designs' men's spokesperson."

"Until a contract is signed regarding the rest of the clothing lines, everything is negotiable." Throwing Devlin's words back at him went down as smoothly as Johnny Walker Blue. "This is a business decision. I'm sure you understand that I have to look out for my best interests."

Silence. Rory waited. He wished he could see the look on Devlin's face. The man wouldn't like being on the disadvantaged side of the negotiation process.

"If I agree to hire Elizabeth, will you sign a contract to act as our spokesperson exclusively for all of our men's clothes?"

"Hire Elizabeth and we'll discuss the issue."

ONCE INSIDE HER town house, Elizabeth kicked off her red pumps and collapsed onto her couch. Not even her ruby slippers had helped with today's interview.

A sadist had to have invented the job search process. That was the only explanation for the torture involved.

She picked up her phone and called Nancy. "How'd the chemo go this week?"

"Not too bad. The new anti-nausea medicine is helping a lot." Nancy's voice sounded much stronger than it had in weeks.

"Thank goodness for modern pharmaceuticals. And congrats. You've passed the halfway mark in your treatment."

"That does feel good. I love the Fight Like a Girl T-shirt you gave me, by the way."

"I thought it was fitting, since you're one of the toughest— and I mean that in a positive way—women I've ever known. You will kick this." Nancy's battle put Elizabeth's job situation into perspective. Her problems were insignificant compared to her friend's. "What time do you want me to bring over the soup from Cohen's Deli?"

"Will six-thirty work?"

"My schedule is wide open."

"Speaking of that, how's the job search going?"

After telling Nancy the job situation was going well, Elizabeth ended her call.

If only the search was going as well as the picture she'd painted for her friend.

The interview she'd had today with a small but stable agency had gone passably well by most standards. Rhea and Kayse primarily dealt with food service companies. Not the best fit, considering Elizabeth's culinary skills, and the salary wouldn't come close to covering her mortgage payment, let alone her other expenses. But she didn't have a lot of options.

The more she interviewed, the less enthusiastic she became. She wanted to choose her clients. The thought of getting people to buy luxuries and useless products to increase sales for huge corporations left her feeling hollow. She wanted to help people like Rory, who needed to increase their family business to pay for life's necessities.

Thinking of him sent an ache chasing through her system. She'd tried to stop this exercise in futility and focus on her future, but everything reminded her of him. Today, when she'd seen him staring down at her from the Times Square billboard, her eyes had teared up, blurring her vision so badly she'd stumbled off the curb.

After her interview she'd transferred money from her emergency savings to cover this month's mortgage payment. Then, after seeing her account balance in stark reality, she'd called a Realtor about putting the town house on the market. If she lived off boxed mac and cheese, ramen noodles and PB&J sandwiches, she could last another two months tops. No getting around the brutal fact that she had to get out from under her mortgage payments. So much for a permanent home.

She inhaled deeply. No big deal. She'd survived before she purchased the town house, she'd survive after she sold it.

Darth Vader's theme rang out from her cell phone. Hell must have frozen over if Devlin was calling. How had she missed that happening when she'd read the paper this morning, and why hadn't she deleted him from her contact list? "Hello, Micah. What a surprise to hear from you."

No kidding. That was like saying snow in June was a surprise.

"I've been reconsidering our working relationship. For cohesiveness's sake, I'd like you to continue being part of the team on the new men's line campaign."

Good thing she was sitting down because otherwise she would've fainted. Yup, hell had definitely frozen over. "You signed with Harms and Finn." Chloe had relayed that bit of information yesterday.

"Jack Finn will be contacting you about a position with them."

Considering how she'd pretty much told Devlin to go to hell the last time they'd talked, the job offer made no sense, setting off Elizabeth's if-something-appears-too-good-to-be-true-it-usually-is radar. "What would my position be?"

"You'd work exclusively coordinating Rory's shoots and appearances."

"Does he know about this?"

The man's silence spoke volumes. Rory knew. Devlin was simply trying to figure out how to spin the truth. He cleared his throat. "When I told Rory we'd signed with another agency, he refused to consider any further ventures if you weren't involved."

While thrilled that Rory cared enough to fight to get her job back, she wanted to land a position on her own merits. She didn't want something handed to her because she was involved with the campaign's model.

But if she accepted the job she could probably keep her town house, and she could see Rory again.

However, accepting Devlin's offer also meant working with pain-in-the-ass clients. She would go back to having no control over her career and convincing people to buy high-priced designer clothes to make themselves feel better instead of concentrating on the things in life that really mattered. Family. Friends. Honesty. Creating a legacy.

And the thought of returning to that life left her cold and surprisingly depressed. She desperately needed more.

Her earlier thoughts flitted through her mind. Small family-owned firms needed, but couldn't afford, quality advertising. Why couldn't she work with people like Rory to increase their business and make their lives better? The idea blossomed within her, leaving her more excited about her career than she'd been in years.

"Micah, while I appreciate your offer, my answer is no, thank you."

A WEEK LATER, Elizabeth stood on the McAlister front porch, her purse full of Claritin, and wished her knees would quit knocking. What if Rory didn't feel the same way she did? After all, he hadn't called her since she'd left Colorado. Maybe he hadn't felt the same connection. Maybe he didn't want a long-term relationship with her. Maybe he didn't love her like she loved him.

But he cared enough to strong-arm Devlin to hire her.

Okay, say he didn't love her. She still had an advantageous business proposal for him. They could both benefit from her advertising suggestions whether they had a personal relationship or not.

Who was she kidding? That would never be enough for her.

"Never thought I'd see you here again."

Her breath caught in her throat at Rory's low, husky voice coming from behind her. With her heart banging against her ribs, she turned to find him standing there on the walkway. He looked almost exactly as he had the day they'd met. Dark blue snap-front shirt, fringed chaps, the crazy royal flush belt buckle and his ever present Stetson. The reality of how much she'd missed him, of how much she loved him, of how much rode on his response to her proposition slammed into her, leaving her weak. "I have a business proposal for you."

"Other than the twenty-five grand I made, our last business deal didn't work out so well. At least the money will get us through a few months."

Since his hat shaded his eyes, she couldn't tell if he was kidding. Didn't matter. She barreled forward. Big gains required big risks. "I'm unemployed, in large part because of you and your stubbornness. The least you can do is hear me out. I think you owe me that."

That's it, Elizabeth, get off to a good start by blaming the guy. That'll make him want to talk to you.

"That didn't come out right." She clutched her briefcase tighter to control her shaking hands. "I'd appreciate the opportunity to present my ideas to you."

His gaze softened as he sauntered toward her. For a minute she thought he might pull her into his arms. She wished he would. That way she'd know he cared.

"Come on in and tell me about this business proposal."

He opened the front door and stepped aside for her to enter. Once inside, the house's warmth and comfort enveloped her. Somehow in the short time she'd spent here, this house had become a home to her, more so than any other place she'd lived.

She walked into the living room and sank onto the couch. Not knowing what else to say, she asked about Nannette's health.

"She's doing better. The oncologist confirmed her collapse was from stress and exhaustion. He's ordered her to take it easier."

"Bet you're having fun trying to get her to follow that order." Elizabeth stared out the window at the mountains, which were so like the man she loved—sturdy, constant, providing shelter to the valleys below.

"Every day or so I lock her in her room so she has to rest."

Elizabeth laughed. She loved his humor, and how he made her smile.

"Mom and Avery are in Portland for another round of treatment. The last CT scan showed her tumor hasn't grown."

"That's wonderful news." Elizabeth took a deep breath and plunged ahead, while she had the courage and he'd given her an opening. "That's part of what brings me here. You need to increase your business to pay for her treatment. I can help you do that." She unzipped her briefcase and pulled out a black binder. Through working on this idea for Rory's ranch, she'd rediscovered what had brought her to the advertising field— the joy of creating something she felt passionate about.

She held out the proposal, and when he failed to take it, she placed it on the coffee table in front of them.

"You haven't been able to find another job?"

"I'm tired of being part of a large agency. I want to choose my clients, and do work that excites me. I want to make a difference for people who need to increase their business to improve their lives."

"Is that why you turned Devlin down?"

"He told you?"

Rory nodded.

"While I appreciate what you did for me, I want to get a job on my own merits."

"I thought that's how you'd feel, but I wanted you to have a choice." Rory picked up the binder and flipped through the pages.

Her gaze remained locked on his hands. Such strong hands, capable of creating such incredible passion. She blushed, remembering what he'd done to her body when they'd made love. And yet his hands could offer such compassion, as they had when she'd been sick.

Suddenly, warmth coursed through her. Damn pheromones. She had to remain clear-headed. Her future was at stake.

Turning her attention to Rory's face, she scrutinized his

features for reactions as he studied her proposal. She hadn't poured bits of herself into a campaign as she had in this one for years. She'd laid out a new website design, coordinated it with an updated brochure, then outlined a marketing strategy.

No reaction. Not good. How could he not love what she'd done?

"I appreciate all the trouble you've gone to, but us working together isn't a good idea."

She ignored the painful twinge in her heart and charged forward, refusing to take no for an answer. "Even if I didn't know how much you dislike dealing with the advertising aspects of your business, looking at your website, your brochures and the ranch's signage would tell me that. If you hire me, I can coordinate those things for you."

"I don't want a business relationship with you."

Her stomach fell and she fought back tears. She hadn't expected such a quick and brutal rejection. "I can increase this ranch's business. I can help you tap into new markets. Give me a chance."

She bit her lip, hating that she danced precariously close to begging.

"You don't get it, Lizzie. I want a personal relationship with you."

Her heart stopped. Just for a second, as his words sank in. She closed her eyes, fearing she was dreaming.

The leather couch scrunched under Rory's movements. When she peeked out from under her lashes, she found him kneeling in front of her. Tears pooled in her eyes.

"You think you could get used to living here?" His large warm hands covered her icy ones.

"I've been exploring the possibilities. I've stocked up on Claritin. I'm considering buying stock in the company." Her gaze remained focused on her ruby slippers. *Please let their magic work this time.*

"Elizabeth." He released her hands. His thumb gently tilted

her chin upward, forcing her gaze to meet his. The look in his eyes, one of tenderness and desire, rendered her speechless. "I want you here. In my house. In my bed. In my life."

"You want us to live together?"

"For a smart businesswoman, you're being awfully dense."

"I'm not being dense. You're being vague."

He flashed her a blinding smile. "I say I want you in my bed and in my life, and that's how you respond?"

"I want to be clear on where you see our relationship going."

"Do I have to spell it out?"

"Apparently."

"I love you. Marry me." His voice wavered the tiniest bit.

Tears stung her eyes. "How can you love me after all I've done? After how I treated you? I looked down on you because I thought you were just a ranch hand, while you treated me with respect. I don't deserve you."

"That doesn't matter now. I can't live without you. Please marry me."

"Yes, I'll marry you."

"Won't you miss the big city?"

"I'd miss you more." Elizabeth smiled. Her cousin Janice had been right. It was amazing what no longer mattered once she found the right man.

Strong hands lifted her. She wrapped her arms around Rory's shoulders as he sank onto the couch, settling her on his lap. He kissed her with a reverence that warmed her all the way to her toes. "There is so much to love about you. You're confident, funny, caring and sexy as hell."

His words reached deep inside her, sewing together the hole in her heart her parents had created. "I love you so much." She looked into his mesmerizing brown eyes. "I'll have to send my cousin Janice a thank-you gift. Coming to her wedding was the best thing that ever happened to me. I'd never have met you otherwise." She bit her lip, deciding to truly test her shoes' magic. "Will you be the Harrington-Smyth Agency's first client? I want to help you increase your business."

"As long as you don't make me model for the ranch's website."

"Are you giving up modeling?"

"I'm finishing out my contract with Devlin for the jeans campaign. He wants me to model other clothing items, but I haven't given him an answer yet. If he kicks in enough bucks I might consider it, but no way in hell am I modeling underwear."

"The women of the world will be so disappointed. What if I need you to model for one of my future clients?"

"No way, sweetheart. The only modeling I'll do is for you in the privacy of our bedroom. There I'll model anything you want."

"Even underwear?"

"Honey, for you I'll model nude."

She chewed on her lower lip and looked him up and down. "I don't know. I'll need to take preliminary photos, kind of like a screen test for a movie."

He stood, still cradling her in his arms. "How about we go upstairs and you can see if you think I'm up for the job."

* * * * *

HEART & HOME

Heartwarming romances where love can
happen right when you least expect it.

COMING NEXT MONTH
AVAILABLE JANUARY 10, 2012

#1385 HIS VALENTINE TRIPLETS
Callahan Cowboys
Tina Leonard

#1386 THE COWBOY'S SECRET SON
The Teagues of Texas
Trish Milburn

#1387 THE SEAL'S PROMISE
Undercover Heroes
Rebecca Winters

#1388 CLAIMED BY A COWBOY
Hill Country Heroes
Tanya Michaels

HARCNM1211

REQUEST YOUR FREE BOOKS!
2 FREE NOVELS PLUS 2 **FREE GIFTS!**

Harlequin

American ★ Romance

LOVE, HOME & HAPPINESS

YES! Please send me 2 FREE Harlequin® American Romance® novels and my 2 FREE gifts (gifts are worth about $10). After receiving them, if I don't wish to receive any more books, I can return the shipping statement marked "cancel." If I don't cancel, I will receive 4 brand-new novels every month and be billed just $4.49 per book in the U.S. or $5.24 per book in Canada. That's a saving of at least 14% off the cover price! It's quite a bargain! Shipping and handling is just 50¢ per book in the U.S. and 75¢ per book in Canada.* I understand that accepting the 2 free books and gifts places me under no obligation to buy anything. I can always return a shipment and cancel at any time. Even if I never buy another book, the two free books and gifts are mine to keep forever.

154/354 HDN FEP2

Name	(PLEASE PRINT)

Address	Apt. #

City	State/Prov.	Zip/Postal Code

Signature (if under 18, a parent or guardian must sign)

Mail to the **Reader Service:**
IN U.S.A.: P.O. Box 1867, Buffalo, NY 14240-1867
IN CANADA: P.O. Box 609, Fort Erie, Ontario L2A 5X3

Not valid for current subscribers to Harlequin American Romance books.

Want to try two free books from another line?
Call 1-800-873-8635 or visit www.ReaderService.com.

* Terms and prices subject to change without notice. Prices do not include applicable taxes. Sales tax applicable in N.Y. Canadian residents will be charged applicable taxes. Offer not valid in Quebec. This offer is limited to one order per household. All orders subject to credit approval. Credit or debit balances in a customer's account(s) may be offset by any other outstanding balance owed by or to the customer. Please allow 4 to 6 weeks for delivery. Offer available while quantities last.

> **Your Privacy**—The Reader Service is committed to protecting your privacy. Our Privacy Policy is available online at www.ReaderService.com or upon request from the Reader Service.
>
> We make a portion of our mailing list available to reputable third parties that offer products we believe may interest you. If you prefer that we not exchange your name with third parties, or if you wish to clarify or modify your communication preferences, please visit us at www.ReaderService.com/consumerschoice or write to us at Reader Service Preference Service, P.O. Box 9062, Buffalo, NY 14269. Include your complete name and address.

HARI1B

Harlequin

SPECIAL EDITION

Life, Love and Family

Karen Templeton

introduces

The FORTUNES *of* TEXAS: Whirlwind Romance

When a tornado destroys Red Rock, Texas, Christina Hastings finds herself trapped in the rubble with telecommunications heir Scott Fortune. He's handsome, smart and everything Christina has learned to guard herself against. As they await rescue, an unlikely attraction forms between the two and Scott soon finds himself wanting to know about this mysterious beauty. But can he catch Christina before she runs away from her true feelings?

FORTUNE'S CINDERELLA

Available December 27th wherever books are sold!

*Brittany Grayson survived a horrible ordeal at the hands
of a serial killer known as The Professional...
who's after her now?*

*Harlequin® Romantic Suspense presents a new installment
in Carla Cassidy's reader-favorite miniseries,*
LAWMEN OF BLACK ROCK.

*Enjoy a sneak peek of
TOOL BELT DEFENDER.*

*Available January 2012
from Harlequin® Romantic Suspense.*

"Brittany?" His voice was deep and pleasant and made
her realize she'd been staring at him openmouthed through
the screen door.

"Yes, I'm Brittany and you must be..." Her mind suddenly went blank.

"Alex. Alex Crawford, Chad's friend. You called him
about a deck?"

As she unlocked the screen, she realized she wasn't
quite ready yet to allow a stranger inside, especially a male
stranger.

"Yes, I did. It's nice to meet you, Alex. Let's walk around
back and I'll show you what I have in mind," she said. She
frowned as she realized there was no car in her driveway.
"Did you walk here?" she asked.

His eyes were a warm blue that stood out against his
tanned face and was complemented by his slightly shaggy
dark hair. "I live three doors up." He pointed up the street to
the Walker home that had been on the market for a while.

"How long have you lived there?"

"I moved in about six weeks ago," he replied as they

walked around the side of the house.

That explained why she didn't know the Walkers had moved out and Mr. Hard Body had moved in. Six weeks ago she'd still been living at her brother Benjamin's house trying to heal from the trauma she'd lived through.

As they reached the backyard she motioned toward the broken brick patio just outside the back door. "What I'd like is a wooden deck big enough to hold a barbecue pit and an umbrella table and, of course, lots of people."

He nodded and pulled a tape measure from his tool belt. "An outdoor entertainment area," he said.

"Exactly," she replied and watched as he began to walk the site. The last thing Brittany had wanted to think about over the past eight months of her life was men. But looking at Alex Crawford definitely gave her a slight flutter of pure feminine pleasure.

Will Brittany be able to heal in the arms of Alex,
her hotter-than-sin handyman…or will a second
psychopath silence her forever? Find out in
TOOL BELT DEFENDER
Available January 2012
from Harlequin® Romantic Suspense
wherever books are sold.

HRSEXP0112